The Alchemist's Theorem:
Sir Duffy's Promise

Margaret R. Chiavetta

Lily,

The Alchemist's Theorem:

Sir Duffy's Promise

There are awesome, fat animals in this book. I hope you enjoy it.

A fantasy novel

Margaret R. Chiavetta

For Brayden

A Pot He Carries

First class alchemist Sir H.U. Duffy started his day normally.
The hardy grey-haired man arrived at his apothecary precisely
at sun's breach, one hour before *A Pot He Carries* opened for
business. He produced the golden key that unlocked the heavy
metalwood door, ever so conscious of the temperamental lock
and key system. Twist left, right, hold and then turn knob
and push. The door creaked open. He paused with his eyes
closed and took a ritual deep breath: earthy mushrooms, dank
feverwood bark, fresh pilgrim's water, and the sweet tang of
dogfly honey. Sir Duffy's heart lightened whenever he stepped
into his shop.

He was sure to dust first, per his usual routine. He knew
all too well the horrors of dust and the havoc it could wreak
on reagents. Sir Duffy flicked his wrist with care, kicking up
small wisps with his feather-brush and catching the clouds
with the sticky surface of a mugpop mushroom — a specimen
that thrived on dust.

Next, Sir Duffy checked the back door for the morning delivery. Without fail the mail person had left him a medium-sized package. He retrieved the wooden box and placed it on the gleaming sorting table. Stenciled on the surface of the box was the sender's name: COLLECTIONS OF TERRA COPIA.

He wedged a metal file into a seam and wrenched the top free. Flipping back the lid revealed a nest of shredded feverwood paper. He removed it pinchfuls at a time, feeling the heat produced by the shreds. After several pinchfuls, a small arm reached out from underneath the nest. Sir Duffy thumped his forehead with the heel of his hand, reproaching himself for not being better prepared, and made off to the shelves. He trotted back to the box with a wooden crate and a small sack of stones that he dumped into it. He tried excavating the creature once more, and after a good deal of hisses and chirps, he managed to clear the paper and reveal a small pup. She was dark and snakish, and began squeaking in tantrum, demanding heat. He picked her up with tender gentleness; she was the size of a wild banana.

The gusselsnuff pup squirmed in his large hands. She had a prognostic snout, black velvet fur with a scaly underbelly, two skinny arms with two forked fingers on each hand, and no hind legs but a fat tail instead. He placed the newborn inside the crate and on top of the burble stones, which naturally produced a very warm heat. The pup quieted at once and curled up amongst the rocks.

"'Ow 'bout I call you Esther, after me grandma?" said Sir Duffy. The pup snorted in her sleep. "She was a great alchemist, you know. She's in the 'istory books!" Esther covered her snout with both hands and curled into herself. "So good to 'ave an Esther 'round 'ere again." He moved the crate into his office and placed it on a metalwood table near the window that overlooked his flourishing garden.

The patch needed watering and mulching, but before he tended to it, he checked his inventory up front to make sure all was in order. Fully stocked shelves lined the four walls of the shop. The racks up against the window showcased the higher-grade items. The rare and more expensive reagents were locked up in a cabinet behind the register. The glass containers varied in shape, size and color. Most were translucent unless the reagent required lightless storage. Tables and tall racks crowded the center area, covered in bottles, jars, brass scales and networks of colorful beakers. Bubbling cauldrons of questionable matter hung over quiet gas flames. Rays of the rising sun shining through the large front windows dashed off the various reflective surfaces. Exotic plants wrapped long limbs around bottles, beakers and table legs. Sir Duffy smiled at the pleasing sight of his organized chaos.

He walked to the front of the shop with a clipboard in hand, and unscrewed lids and uncorked bottles, being sure to sniff and sometimes taste reagents for spoilage. He used a spray bottle hooked to his belt for dampening certain products, such as red silk moss and pepper mold. He unfolded a utility knife and produced a tiny pair of clippers and snipped off the dying leaves of a miniature paraffin bush. He examined every shelf in a speedy, much practiced manner and finished with a sigh of satisfaction.

After donning an apron, he continued to the back garden. Though it was small, the plants were fruitful and yielded plenty of stock for Sir Duffy's inventory. It was the beginning of spring, and the patch overflowed with young plants. He had switched out the spray bottle of water for one filled with manic weasel urine, which did wonders for babylump bushes and gargoyle vines. Then he grabbed a sack of ground horse fangs—a hard-to-come-by item that did considerable good for pollypig flowers and tigerblood bushes—and spread a handful over the soil. He sprayed, dusted, watered, clipped and collected his plants, muttering encouragement in the foreign words his grandma Esther had taught him. After some laboring his work was done, and he took his basket of collected items into the shop and placed them on the sorting table.

"I'll leave 'em for Mendel to sort," he mumbled.

As he washed the dirt off his hands in the water basin, he heard the front door creak open and assumed it was Mendel, his very young apprentice. He removed his apron after drying his hands. "Oi! Mendel! What good is 'avin' the key to the back if you're not goin' to use it?" There was no response, but Sir Duffy knew Mendel was a quiet boy. "Your shoes best not be muddy!"

Still no response.

Suspicious, Sir Duffy went to the front of the store. He was surprised to see a tall, thin man in a long, dark grey coat standing at the register. "Oh, sorry mister, I wasn't expectin' customers. The store isn't quite open yet. Somefin' I can 'elp you wif?"

"Sir Hennasee Ulfric Duffy of The Living Arts Academy, I presume?" The gaunt gentleman extended a ghoulish hand. Sir Duffy shook it.

"Aye . . . that'd be me. You are . . . ?" Sir Duffy released the gentleman's hand and moved so that the register counter was between them.

"I am Don Horus Clapstone of the Academy of Advanced Disciplines. It is a pleasure to meet you. I have heard so much about you during my inquiries. Though no one mentioned that you were a Northern Forester."

"Oh, I left the Forests wif me grandma when I was ten, but never left the accent." The alchemist laughed uncomfortably. "What inquiries would me name turn up in, might I ask?" Sir Duffy felt uneasy just at the sight of this gentleman, but hearing he was a Don, the title earned from the Academy of Advanced Disciplines, made him even more apprehensive. The AAD was an overshadowing institution to Sir Duffy's own LAA, and there was much opposition between the two.

"Nothing at all malicious, Sir. I'm merely an enthusiastic collector of rare items from the Old Regime Era. There is one very rare item in particular I am in search of on behalf of our Regula. I've been reading about this particular item in *The Dark Days of The Old Regime,* and after much inquiry I was directed towards Regime alchemy . . . which in turn led me to you, here in Abylant."

Sir Duffy stiffened and felt his heart hammering in his chest. The Dark Days were a very serious, nearly catastrophic time for the continent of Terra Copia. It ended the Old Regime Era, a harmonious period until *the mistake,* and started the Regula Era, which restricted many of the old freedoms that were allegedly the cause of the event. Sir Duffy wasn't sure what Don Clapstone could possibly want to collect from the Dark Days that wouldn't cause serious trouble, but he hoped that he wasn't looking for a particular item that Sir Duffy knew about all too well.

"I'm sure I can't 'elp you wif anyfin' involvin' the dark days, Don. Me alchemy practices are well wifin the laws of Regula, though I maintain as much of the Old Regime as I can," replied Sir Duffy.

"I assure you, I am not here to police you. I am here only to help protect our world. The item I seek would be secured safely. I have a certificate of approval from our Regula that allows me to collect this item." Don Clapstone reached into his jacket and produced a rolled-up sheaf of paper and handed it to Sir Duffy. "I know since it is illegal to possess this item that it is unlikely the owner would broadcast his or her possession of it. However, I was told by a number of people that you may know where to direct me."

Sir Duffy unrolled the document carefully and read the inscription:

Official Regula Document DS103
From the offices of Defensive Sciences

I, Melana Wildrew, Secretary of Defensive Sciences for our beloved Regula, do hereby grant one Don Horus Clapstone, of The Academy of Advanced Disciplines, permission to seek out and collect the unlawful item of the Dark Days known as Putrid's Heart. Since the only known antidote to the curse of Putrid's Heart is another Putrid's Heart, we feel it is of the utmost importance to have one in the possession of the Regula as a means to counteract any future curse set upon us by unknown enemies.

For the love of Regula and Terra Copia,
Melana Wildrew

Sir Duffy went cold and pale. No one comfortably spoke of this item since the rise of the Regula. Alchemy was seriously threatened during the establishment of the new government, but survived because while alchemy conjured the great evil, alchemy also cast it back into the depths.

"Well, Don, there isn't much I can tell you that isn't already written in books. Putrid's 'eart is so rare cos of where it comes from and what is required to retrieve it. I'm sure you've read that only an ore badger can retrieve this item, and no one's seen one for quite some time."

Ore badgers were small, silver creatures that lived underground. They had long bodies covered in steel-like scales. Their front feet were metal-ish, shovel-shaped claws. They had no eyes, and a cone-shaped snout. These creatures were built for digging, and no one was quite sure how deep into the earth they could burrow until *the mistake* happened. The badgers tended to bring up different kinds of ore to construct nests within the roots of trees.

"The investigators of *the mistake*," continued Sir Duffy, "figured out that a female ore badger brought up just a couple Putrid's 'earts for 'er nest, near the base of Blackburn Volcano, but there 'ave been no sightings of an ore badger since *the reckoning*. Poor beasts were 'unted relentlessly." Sir Duffy paused. He hoped this would satisfy Don Clapstone, but the Don just held an unyielding stare that told him to continue.

"A female ore badger burrowed deep enough to come across a couple of these 'earts." Sir Duffy spoke slightly dazed, as though he was talking from a great distance. "A traveler came across the nest and collected the unusual ore and sold it to merchants. One of the stones made it into the 'ands of the alchemist

7

we all know as Sir Charles Mostly, who experimented wif it, eventually conjurin' the great evil by mistake.

"Sir Mostly 'eroically took responsibility for 'is mistake," said Sir Duffy proudly, "and was able to determine from 'is meticulous research that another Putrid's 'eart could banish the great evil back into the planet's core. But not 'avin' another 'eart in possession, 'e assembled the famous team, made up of two alchemists, includin' 'imself, and three adventurers. They searched the entire continent, eventually findin' out 'bout the nest. They found one stone located some ways from it, and 'e was able to call the creature away. At great costs, though," he said sadly. "Many people 'ave returned to the site but never found another Putrid's 'eart." Sir Duffy let out a sigh, and the glaze in his eyes faded. He felt very tired and very sad.

"Thank you for confirming what I have gathered so far, Sir Duffy. I have already searched the original site at Blackburn Volcano, and like so many others, found nothing. However, the accounts say that the original traveler took an uncertain number of the stones, but Sir Charles only came across two. Therefore, there are likely one or two stones in someone's possession. I feel that finding this person is my best chance. I've come to you because of your connection to the famous team. I wonder if you are privy to any information that the team may have acquired during their travels?" Sir Duffy kept a cool gaze on Don Clapstone, but inside he felt a shock of panic.

"Sorry, Don. But me grandma rarely ever spoke of *the mistake* afterward, and I only 'ad two more years wif 'er before she passed on. She was of an older age when she set out on the journey, and the ordeal took a lot out of 'er. She was never the same. If she 'ad that information she never passed

8

it on to me." Sir Duffy breathed deeply through his nose. He wanted this discussion to end, but he knew he would have to give Don Clapstone something before he would leave. "The only mention she made of the ordeal was a pleasant memory she 'ad of the town of Jordstrum, just over the lip of Madder Valley. There was a family that took 'em in. They 'ad beautiful children, and the daughter was very interested in alchemy. But that's all she ever mentioned." Sir Duffy frowned; he missed his grandmother.

"Jordstrum, you say?" The Don looked eager. "That town has not been mentioned during my inquiries. What was the name of the family?" Don Clapstone seemed to accept this information as helpful to his cause, but Sir Duffy wanted to make sure it was enough. It was necessary to reveal the name.

"The Bellamues, I fink."

The Don reached into his jacket and produced paper and ink pen. He quickly jotted down the family name and town.

"Thank you, Sir Duffy. I have made little progress these last months. This new information has revitalized my hopes." He placed the paper and official document back in his jacket.

"No trouble at all. Will that be all, Don?" Sir Duffy wished to never see this man again.

"Perhaps I will send my colleague later today for some supplies. Even though I have dedicated myself to the Advanced Disciplines, I cannot disregard the powers of Old Regime alchemy like many of my peers do."

"Well, that's good to 'ear," said Sir Duffy. He flinched. The AAD was highly opposed to the ways of the Old Regime and were continuously pressuring the Regula to ban more and more practices. Recently, the institution had launched efforts for the Potions Oversight Act that would force Sir Duffy to have his work monitored by a Regula agent, most likely someone from the AAD. Luckily, members of his own institution, the Living Arts Academy, were fighting the act quite effectively. But the Advanced Disciplines were always looking for ways to dismantle the Living Arts institutions.

Sir Duffy walked Don Clapstone to the door, but the man paused to say more.

"One last thing, Sir Duffy. The rumors go back and forth about Sir Mostly's journal, the only documentation of his experiments with the heart. Most say it went with him, but some say it still survives. Would you contest this rumor for me? Did Esther Duffy say whether or not she was ever in possession of it?" This was a very bold question for Don Clapstone to ask. Sir Duffy suddenly felt the live danger that this man presented.

"As far as she knew, it was destroyed."

"That's what I thought." Don Clapstone's eyes flicked towards the locked cabinet behind the register. Then he turned and left the shop.

Sir Duffy sat for a moment. His nerves were always easily rattled. The clock hanging above the door had two golden arms stretched opposite one another across a smooth black slate surface. One hand was a small blaze of sunlight and the other was a soft silver glow of moonlight. The clock said that the shop had been open a short while. Thankfully, there weren't any customers yet, and Sir Duffy jumped from his stupor to make a simmerup tonic to restore his nerves.

He put a kettle of water over a small gas flame and flipped over a clean teacup. The flame licked the metal underbelly while Sir Duffy plucked a soggy butterfig from a jar and took a pinchful of powdered pixie's blood from a wooden bowl, tossing them into a stone mortar. Using a burble stone pestle, he massaged the reagents into a warm, fragrant paste and scraped it into his teacup.

The kettle notified him that the water was hot, and it bellowed clouds of steam. He turned off the flame and poured the boiling water over the oily clump, letting it steep. While the paste dissolved, he muttered old, foreign words his grandmother taught him for this remedy. *"Vivame su toteme, vivame su toteme."* The liquid was now a shimmering amber color and had a tangy-sweet smell. Sir Duffy swirled the mixture three times, tipped the cup into his mouth and swallowed all in one gulp. There was a metallic aftertaste from the pixie's blood, and the sweet scent of the butterfig filled his nose. Then, like the sun appearing through a break in a rough storm, a warm pulse began to emit from his beating heart, and he felt his body relax. Sir Duffy cleaned up, relieved by the restoration of his rattled nerves.

The slow whine of the back door's hinges crept into the front room, and Sir Duffy was pleased to hear the low shuffle of Mendel's feet. He walked to the back room and saw the boy sorting the items from the garden. Sir Duffy found the sight so comforting that for the moment he forgot about the troublesome inquiry and the decisions he had to make.

"Morning, Sir H." Mendel's voice was quiet and soft. He was skinny and pale. A mop of black hair fell into his deep-set, angular eyes. Sir Duffy noticed the boy was rocking slightly back and forth while picking pollypig buds from the basket. He understood the boy's repetitive movements, small twitches and thinking habits well. It's how he had identified Mendel's ancestral significance.

The alchemist knew that the uncontrollable gestures were an indication of what was going on inside Mendel's head. Rocking kept him from feeling trapped in a body he sometimes couldn't control. The type and degree of rocking reflected his level of uneasiness. Mendel was swaying gently from foot to foot, which meant that the boy was looking forward to something.

"Good to see you Mendel! Straight to work, what a good lad you are." Sir Duffy smiled. "Want to see the newest treasure to arrive?"

Mendel stopped rocking, looked up and dropped the pollypig buds.

"Ha! Thought you would. She's in me office. Come on." Sir Duffy entered the office and reached into the crate, muttering in a gentle voice. The alchemist saw the boy's eyes go wide at the sight of the small, wiggling creature.

"A gusselsnuff! I knew she'd arrive today. The merchant said the end of the month, but I knew I knew because she's small and she's a spring animal and it's the beginning of the season and they'd get her through the capital faster." Mendel inched forward. Esther sniffed the air; her hands gripped Sir Duffy's finger, and the end of her tail searched around for its own grip, not quite prehensile yet.

"Go on, then. Give 'er a pat. Let 'er smell you first," said Sir Duffy.

Mendel tapped his forehead twice with his fingers and then breathed on them. The boy did this whenever he handled a specimen or reagent for the first time, and the alchemist reckoned the familiar sensations helped him differentiate the new one. Mendel lowered his hand and reached for the pup's head, pausing just above her nose, letting her sniff and gently lick his fingers. He stroked her cheek and smiled at the smoothness of her virgin fur. Esther stretched her neck and purred in response to the affection.

"This is Esther. I'll teach you 'ow to make 'er a right fine mash. And we can carry 'er 'round wif us, once 'er tail is strong enough to 'old onto fings."

"Is it a meatyweed mash, with dogfly larvae?" Mendel swayed from foot to foot, beaming with enthusiasm.

"Right you are, Mendel. Where'd you learn 'bout the mash?"

"I read about it in the book you lent me, *Managing Your Reagents*. We're going to need doglfy larvae." The boy's expression changed, and he had a faraway look in his eyes. Sir Duffy knew he was off somewhere in his head, making the mash.

Mendel absently tugged on Esther's tail, which she didn't seem to mind, but then his sleeve fell back and exposed a dark purple bruise across his forearm. Sir Duffy frowned, and the boy's eyes returned from contemplation and noticed the exposed bruise. He shrugged his shoulders. "I made my father unhappy again." He stared at Esther's tail. "Going without dinner was worse than the slap." The boy repetitively brushed nothing away from his thigh. It had taken Sir Duffy a while to figure out what this gesture meant. Mendel was feeling isolated and alone.

Sir Duffy's heart broke. He sighed and gave the boy a reassuring smile. "Well, 'ow 'bout you see if you can mix up your own icy clot poultice and leech tea, if you can remember. And I 'ave a jar of pickled pears on me desk if you're still 'ungry."

Mendel immediately brightened. He let go of Esther's tail and skipped out of the office. After putting the gusselsnuff back in her crate, Sir Duffy bustled to the front of the shop. He watched as the boy threw on his apron and shuffled around the store collecting reagents. The young apprentice counted out arctic cubes and used a brass scale to weigh pinchfuls of chopped cherry twigs. Then he seized a bottle of slug oil and deposited the items on the alchemy table where Sir Duffy had made his tonic. He left them piled to one side and went back for another run. He grabbed two dried swamp leeches, two soggy butterfigs and a vial full of dogfly honey, and flipped on the gas flame underneath the kettle.

Mendel surveyed the table. He used his pointer finger to write symbols in the air and calculate the proportions of the potion. Then with a sharp nod of satisfaction, he grabbed the bottle of slug oil. "First I put two drops of slug oil in the bottom, *then* I grind the cubes on top."

"Good lad!" Sir Duffy always noticed how Mendel never gestured involuntarily when he made potions. He was still in awe of the boy's ability to make a potion correctly after being shown only once.

After crushing the cubes, the boy added more slug oil to form a wet powdery mixture. Next he put the chopped cherry twigs in his mouth and chewed. Sir Duffy could smell sweet blossoms in the air. The boy spat them out into the bowl, and folded the twigs into the wet powder. He dumped the batch on a square of spongy cloth which he twisted into a bundle and set aside. The kettle whistled, so he turned off the flame and flipped over a clean teacup. His cheeks were flushed and his eyes were bright. Next, Mendel ground the dried leeches into a powder and mashed them together with the butterfigs. He scraped the glob into the teacup, pouring the hot water over it. As it steeped, he quietly said, "*Vivame su solele,*" which Sir Duffy translated under his breath. "Heal my body."

Mendel completed the tea with a few drops of dogfly honey, swirled it four times and drank quickly. He rolled up his sleeve and placed the poultice over his bruise, wincing at the chill, but then smiled as the tea did its work.

"Well done, my boy!" Sir Duffy clapped his hands. The boy had an accomplished grin on his face.

They both heard the front door open, and Sir Duffy could see a bald head poking up from behind one of the racks. "Why don't you finish doin' that in me office, and eat some pears while you wait, then sort the rest of the basket." Mendel made off with a skip to the back of the shop.

"Oi! Gurrant, is that you? Wife snorin' again?"

Mendel wanted to eat four pears, but that would leave an odd number in the jar so he only ate three, sharing one with Esther. She nibbled on small chunks of sour fruit while sitting in her species' natural S-shape. The boy followed the curve of her stance with his pointer finger and admired the symmetry. She purred in response.

By the time he finished eating and playing with the gusselsnuff, the dark bruise on his arm had been replaced with a small yellow splotch. The sight of the healing wound kept *the thought* from crawling up his leg. This creature-of-a-thought was something he kept far away from his mind, down by his feet. It was menacing, and often clawed its way up his leg, trying to voice its troublesome worries, so he often had

to bat it away. *The thought* tried to convince him of things, things that made him feel desperate and panicked. Like his existence made other people unhappy, and that he wasn't actually human and if anyone found out they'd run him out of town. His best effort was required to keep *the thought* away.

The art and precision of alchemy did just that because it demanded Mendel's best. Getting to know the makeup of individual reagents required his undivided curiosity, which was a rather restless voice in his head that never stopped asking questions. The unchanging laws of alchemical mathematics were like glue that stuck to his memory permanently, unlike the ever-changing nature of human interaction that bounced more often than stuck. This was a source of great anxiety for Mendel that made him susceptible to *the thought*, but when a potion successfully came to life, he felt a rush of euphoria that swept all of his worries away.

Before Mendel found alchemy, he was completely unaware of his ability to feel happy. Now he spent every second he could in *A Pot He Carries* with his only human friend Sir H. and the many friends that lined the shelves and tables.

Mendel finished sorting, processing and storing the items from the collecting basket, making sure that all of the jars and containers had an even number of specimens. He usually ate the odd numbers if their chemical makeup allowed for it, otherwise he went to the garden and picked another when Sir H. wasn't looking.

Skipping to the front of the shop, he overheard Lady Mickle, the owner of the local inn and restaurant, telling Sir H. about a chronic pain in her left eye. Eye spasms call for a blinking spice potion. In anticipation, the boy dashed toward a corner shelf for a jar of ginger pearls. But Mendel heard the woman say the pain happened only at night. He froze and quickly drew golden symbols—that only he could see—in the air with his pointer finger. This helped him summon the right memory. Bucking roses were in season and only bloomed at night. The eye pain was an allergy. He changed directions and snatched a tall bottle of wild citrus tree sap from a table and popped it into Sir H.'s front apron pocket.

Quite often he was right when anticipating a needed remedy, but when he was unsure of how to treat a customer's complaint, he followed his mentor around the shop and caught whatever items Sir H. tossed at him. He always mentally catalogued what solutions the alchemist prescribed to which problems with the proper mental glue.

People arrived and departed at a steady rhythm, and Mendel tried to listen carefully to the educational conversations that Sir H. had with the more advanced patrons, though he was easily distracted when the sunlight hit a bottle in a particularly beautiful way.

". . . you 'ave to mix 'em at night but don't add 'em to this til mornin', and don't drink til after lunch . . . "

". . . best way to bleed a pixie is to just cut the 'eads off and let 'em drain into a bowl. Save the wings, they're good for fevers . . . "

Mendel traced a golden equation in the air and knew the former was a potion for treating deafness, but he hadn't learned about processing pixies yet. They were nasty little creatures about the size of an adult's forearm. They lived in treetops and built makeshift villages by stringing vines and branches together. Their skin was rough and resembled tree bark, and their limbs were long, spindly branches used for jab-bing. They buzzed through the air with cellophane wings and usually traveled in swarms, devastating crops and orchards during the raiding season. During that time of year, Sir H. treated many venomous pixie bites, which festered quickly and could be fatal if left untreated. Mendel traced the sym-bols used for desiccating pixies' blood in the air, attached the knowledge to his general pixie equation and then stuck it back in his memory. He learned a good deal from eavesdropping and observation.

Mendel loved growing his knowledge, and felt anxious about the very idea of idle thought. Thinking about and imag-ining what-ifs, cause and effect, and solutions to problems kept his attention away from bad thoughts. Whenever he retreated inside his head to think, he paced the room. Walking around helped him navigate his mind, which had been his greatest challenge since birth. Most of the time he was unaware of his pacing, and only noticed when he heard Sir H.'s pleasant chuckle, a comforting noise that helped Mendel forget to feel self-conscious. The boy's previous teachers often punished him for his thinking habits by tying his ankle to the desk.

Before Mendel met Sir H. his education was more like his damnation. Mendel was always eager to learn about Terra Copia, and he wanted nothing more than to know whatever there was to know. But his parents, teachers and the other children of the village schoolhouse treated him as though he were sick, as though his habits and difficulties were symptoms of an incurable disease.

His struggle began with his first memory: his mother repeat-edly made the same noise and the same gesture over and over while getting angrier and angrier as Mendel watched her with curious eyes. Eventually his mother threw what was in her hand across the room and left the boy alone. He had a few similar memories of his mother before she left one day and never came back.

The thought first crawled forth from its dark origins during his second year at school. Its raspy voice sounded from a lightless, cold place that Mendel never saw but felt. The teachers did much of the same as his parents, repeating what it was they wanted him to learn over and over. But back then Mendel's thoughts were so hard to control and navigate that he often wouldn't realize what people were saying until they were quite angry. He was punished regularly, and knew the far corner of the school room well. That corner was where he first heard the voice of *the thought*.

Why aren't you ever with your own kind? it asked. *How strange it is for a human to spend so little time with other humans.* Its voice became louder and more articulate over time, distracting Mendel a great deal, making it even harder for him to learn. It was *the thought* that pointed out how unhappy he made other people. All of his attention went towards keeping *the thought* down by his foot and away from his mind.

Eventually *the thought* convinced him that he was too sick to learn. He went to school less and less, and one day stopped altogether. No notices were sent home, as though the teachers had agreed with *the thought*. Since his mother had already left and his father didn't pay any attention to his whereabouts, he felt no reason to go back to school.

Staying home wasn't much better. To occupy his thoughts, Mendel spent the days wandering the rolling green hills and patches of woodland that surrounded the town of Abylant. Nature quickly became his friend. She was delightfully distracting and very inviting. Every wild thing begged for his attention. He often ran from plant to plant, dazzled by the variety of colors. He chased after painted insects or furry creatures that scuttled down holes or up trees. Nature never made him feel as though he didn't belong. In fact, Mendel felt as though he were allowed to be himself out in the forest. *The thought* never had much to say while he was discovering the land on his own.

A lake lay in a valley two hills north of Abylant. Mendel routinely hiked there in the morning and fished for breakfast. Before his father had given up on him, he had taught Mendel how to catch, clean and eat a raw fish. It was the only thing he had ever learned from his father. There was something about the simplicity of the procedure that made it easy for Mendel to remember. A stick and string, a hook and bait, a body of water and hungry fish. Once he experienced the pleasure of catching and eating his first fish, he never forgot how to do it. The routine helped him figure out that procedures were an easy way for him to remember things.

Breakfast was usually followed by a bath, depending on the weather. During the colder season he just splashed water on his face, but nicer weather made for a great swim. By the time he finished eating and bathing, only the morning passed. There was plenty of daylight left, so Mendel explored the land. He developed a keen eye for landmarks, which kept him from getting lost. His favorite site was a giant fallen metalwood tree. Raindrops clinked against the trunk and echoed a symphony. Such sounds soothed him.

Once he had mentally mapped out the surrounding land, he found more time on his hands. Needing something to do, he took to scrutinizing the different plants and wildlife. He wondered why certain plants were a certain color or why some of the ugliest looking vegetation smelled so nice. One day, he was about to eat a brown mushroom that smelled like bread when he heard a voice behind him.

"Oi! I wouldn't eat that, boy! Unless you want the worst belly ache of your life." Sir H. was holding a clump of red silk moss when Mendel first met him.

"Really? What's wrong with it?"

"Well nofin's *wrong* wif it. In fact, it's a great antiseptic for wounds, but it surely will mess up your gut if you eat it."

"What's an ant-peptic? And why does it smell like bread if it's not for eating?" Mendel frowned at the big brown lump-of-a-mushroom.

"Antiseptic . . . means it kills germs that cause infections, and it smells good cos it wants to be eaten, that's 'ow it spawns. It's called weasel gut mushroom." Sir H. chuckled. But then he appeared struck by something. "Oi, what you doin' out 'ere anyway? Why aren't you in school?"

"I don't go to school," was Mendel's simple answer.

"Why's that then?"

Mendel felt *the thought* creeping up his leg and tried to brush it away. "I'm too sick to learn anything. Teachers don't want me there."

Sir H. looked down at the boy's leg and studied him for a moment and then said, "Havin' a brain that works different don't mean you're sick, boy. Just means some people don't understand such a fing. It's the Advanced Disciplines curriculum that don't allow for differences. You're actually a very rare kind of person. Not many like you 'round anymore."

For a moment Mendel felt as though the man could see *the thought* on his leg, intimidating it and making the loathsome creature retreat from observation. He couldn't help turning over the words "rare kind of person" in his mind.

"Do your parents know you're out 'ere?" asked Sir H.

Mendel returned his attention to the man with the round belly. "My father says my mother lives in Demenchi. She's happy there. And my father is Gregory MacKeenie."

Sir H. nodded with understanding. "I see. So you're MacKeenie's boy?" The two of them stood in awkward silence for a moment.

"Why don't you sound like other people?" Mendel raised an eyebrow at him.

Sir H. smiled. "I'm originally from the Northern Forests. We were an isolated bunch before the pioneering days two 'undred years ago. So we speak a little differently."

"Huh." Mendel frowned with his eyebrow still raised. Then he looked over the landscape and another question came to him. "Do you know why that flower over there changes color?"

And that is when the partnership had begun between him and the alchemist. Mendel started coming around the shop, asking all sorts of questions, usually bringing with him an assortment of plants he collected from the forest. He often burst through the door and paced the room while rambling about his observations and hypotheses. Sir H. welcomed the eagerness and encouraged his education in alchemy. He smiled while watching Mendel pace through the shop, waiting patiently for him to run out of energy so the alchemist could impart useful knowledge.

It wasn't long before Sir H. told him about the academy. "You know, Mendel, you don't need your schoolin' 'ere in Abylant in order to be accepted into the academy's School of Alchemy. If you apprentice wif me til you're thirteen and prepare for the entrance exam, well I reckon good marks and a letter from me would get you into the school for sure. Especially given 'ow well your kind does at the academy."

Mendel's eyes widened. He was ten years old at the time, and even though three years seemed like ages, he felt thrilled with the prospect of attending alchemy school. Sir H. explained how Mendel would be able to learn the way he wanted to and not be given a hard time for it. A handful of alchemists at the academy were just like him. Sir H. called them Primores, a kind of rare people Mendel didn't fully understand yet.

"You won't need money to pay for school like 'em Advanced Disciplines students do, but you 'ave to volunteer your time in 'elping to sustain the community. You'll love workin' for me friend Sir Brandiheart. 'E's got acres of greenhouse that are burstin' wif rare and unusual reagents. It'd be great work for you, being a *garden worm*." Sir H. chuckled and explained to Mendel how that was the nickname Sir Brandiheart had given him.

"You really think I can get in, Sir H.? Would I be able to live there?" Mendel's heart leapt at Sir H.'s affirming nod.

The alchemist added, "And I reckon I'll finally accept that teachin' position they've been offerin' me every year. Business isn't as good in the city as it used to be, but I do miss the campus."

Almost two years had passed, and Mendel spent every moment he could in *A Pot He Carries*. He learned everything from growing and harvesting specimens to mixing and brewing potions to organizing and deciphering the mathematics of alchemy. Most importantly, he learned how to better navigate his mind. Next year, he and Sir H. would move to Manuva.

Now, with an ever-present undercurrent of excitement for the future, Mendel inspected and topped off containers with a smile on his face while Sir H. tended to a bubbling caldron.

The front door opened and two individuals entered the shop. Mendel positioned himself behind the register, waiting to see if he could assist Sir H. A tall woman with short black hair stood by the door with a teenage girl at her side. Mendel didn't recognize either of them. Both wore perfectly tailored, long dark grey coats. He had never seen such stylish clothes in Abylant. The woman wore her hair fashionably angled. The young girl had close-cropped red hair and a pale freckled face.

"You must be Don Clapstone's people." Sir H. greeted them with the same voice he used when speaking to the very few townspeople he didn't like. "I can tell from your Advanced Disciplines attire."

"How observant—" muttered the girl, but the woman cut her off with a stern look.

"Yes, how do you do? Sir Duffy, is it?" The woman extended her hand. "I am Don Marriami Woolstrum and this is my student, Pfeifer Logan." Sir H. shook both their hands.

"Pleasure. I *am* Sir Duffy and over there is me apprentice, Mendel MacKeenie." Don Woolstrum nodded at Mendel pleasantly while Pfeifer examined him with a furrowed brow. He looked away and down at their shiny boots.

"Charmed," replied the Don. Mendel thought she was pretty, her sharp features softened by smooth skin. She had perfect posture and stood rigidly with her hands clasped behind her back; Pfeifer did the same but seemed less practiced.

"Well, what can we get for you?" Sir H. seemed nervous to Mendel. His hands were fidgeting with the front of his apron. This made Mendel feel nervous, too.

"I have a list of items we'll need for our travels to Jordstrum. Don Clapstone made the list. I unfortunately am ill-educated on Old Regime alchemy." She tried to sound polite, but Mendel felt that her voice was strained. She produced a folded sheaf of paper and handed it to Sir H., who looked over the items.

"Right . . . right . . . yes. Well, I've got all these." Sir H. beckoned to Mendel who moved promptly to his side. "Gather and package all 'em ones 'cept for the last two, I'll get 'em from the lock up." Mendel took the list, scanned it once and then set off around the shop carrying a small wicker basket on his arm.

While he filled the basket, Sir H. went to the cabinet behind the counter, and the Don and Pfeifer followed him closely. He pulled a silver key on a chain from underneath his shirt, muttered a phrase quietly and turned the key back and forth several times before the cupboard popped open. Both the woman and girl were peering over Sir H.'s shoulder and examining the contents of the cabinet. The alchemist allowed the door to swing open, letting the strangers look into his special stock, while removing the two items needed to complete the order. Mendel was still learning about the reagents in the locked cabinet, so he listened carefully while gathering his part of the list.

"Now, I'm sure Don Clapstone knows what to do wif these two reagents, since 'e's asking for 'em, but I'll leave instructions wif you, Don Woolstrum, just in case." Sir H. placed two medium-sized vials of cloudy gray liquid and two small, sooty-looking eggs on the counter. "Combinin' these will cure any poison. Problem is, you 'ave to wait five minutes after it's mixed in order for it to work. Some poisons will kill you in less than that." Sir H. smiled, but Don Woolstrum returned a slight frown. Pfeifer continued to look over the cabinet.

"Now, these are mountain raven eggs that nest on volcanic ridges. I'll put 'em in a protective case for you. And these are vials of coal cave water, from an 'ot spring deep wifin the caverns of the coal caves of Brugersfield." Sir H. pulled out a small box and placed the two eggs on the cushion inside. "What you do is, crack the egg into the vial and gently swirl it exactly sixty times, no less, and then let it stand for five minutes and then drink. After twenty minutes the potion's useless. The effects will take time, dependin' on the strength of the poison. I 'eard a story 'bout a man, a Regula advisor, who'd been poisoned wif catfink venom, very powerful stuff. They gave 'im this 'ere reverserator antidote after five minutes but they thought it was too late, pronounced 'im dead. 'Alf a day later 'e woke up, 'bout to be autopsied." Sir H. laughed. Don Woolstrum's laugh was delayed and short.

Sir H. closed and locked the cabinet, muttering something under his breath again while jerking the key back and forth. Mendel brought his basketful of reagents to the alchemy table and began to sort the items. He examined them for purity, and mentally noted uses for each one. They were mostly wound treatment, illness healing and prevention reagents, but Mendel also noticed he was packaging elder snake rot and nymph spider's web, which, when mixed together over heat in a vehicle solution, created a rather nasty poison called brain rot, which caused the imbiber to go temporarily mad.

"When you've finished, Mendel, give the package to Pfeifer," said Sir H.

Mendel tied a string around the package and handed it to her, avoiding eye contact. When she flipped open her satchel, something caught his eye—a hunk of metal ore with scratches on the surface. Pfeifer caught him looking and scowled. Mendel brushed at his leg, and the girl stared at him with confusion. He turned away and busied himself by cleaning up the alchemy table.

Sir H. punched the worn keys of the register. "All right, that will be fifty-eight copper pieces and five silver bits." Don Woolstrum handed him a ruby coin, which was equivalent to ten gold pieces. Sir H.'s eyes widened at the sight of the glittering coin.

"Please, Sir Duffy, do not bother with making change. This is complementary of Don Clapstone." Don Woolstrum smiled pleasantly, temporarily melting away her colder expression.

Mendel heard Sir H. clear his throat, and saw a bead of sweat roll down his temple.

"Well, tell the Don that is very 'andsome of 'im. I can offer you more reagents in exchange—"

The Don shook her head before he could finish. "That won't be necessary. We leave tomorrow and we have more than enough supplies. Don Clapstone has an enthusiasm for your line of work that no one in our department seems to appreciate. He considers you a . . . sort of . . . comrade." She smiled again.

"Well, I am quite pleased to 'ear that, Don." Mendel heard hesitation in Sir H.'s voice. "Ah, what department is it you belong to?"

"The School of Defensive Science. We work closely with our Regula to ensure the safety of Terra Copia, which is the reason for our current quest."

"Is our world in danger of another—" Sir H. hesitated again, his temples moist "—another *mistake?*" His hands were clasped together on the counter, knuckles white with tension.

"My dear Sir Duffy." She reached out and gently touched his hands. "Our quest is only proactive in nature. Please do not feel alarmed by our presence or purpose." She smiled warmly and released his hands.

"Well, that's very reassurin', Don," said Sir H. Mendel could tell he didn't mean it.

"Horus says you are a Northern Forester," said Don Woolstrum.

"Yes. Well, I left the region when I was a boy. Went to stay wif me grandma at the alchemy campus in Manuva."

"Do you ever go back? I have to admit, I have always been a little curious about the Northern Forests."

"I 'aven't been back in years, but I see Foresters now and then. They usually catch me up on the gossip back 'ome."

Her laugh sounded more genuine this time. "Well, we should be going. Perhaps our paths will cross again."

"Perhaps, Don Woolstrum. It's been a pleasure doin' business." Mendel watched Sir H. escort her and Pfeifer toward the door. "If you fink of anyfin' else you need before you go, please come by again."

"Thank you so much for your services, Sir Duffy. It has been a pleasure meeting you and your apprentice." The Don let her chilly exterior melt away one last time, giving a full smile that revealed her very straight teeth. Mendel blushed and Sir H. continued to sweat.

"Bye then." Sir H. shut the door behind them, leaned against it and let out a long sigh. He looked at Mendel, examining him closely and wiping his graying temples with his sleeve. "You're twelve years now, right Mendel?"

"Yes, Sir H.," answered Mendel proudly.

"Hmph. Old enough I'd say. Watch the store for me, would you Mendel?" He didn't wait for a reply, and disappeared into the back room.

Mendel noticed the odd changes in Sir H.'s behavior, but assured himself that grownups always seemed to have a reasonable explanation for their unusual behaviors. He turned his attention to tidying up the shop.

Sir Duffy bustled into his office and poured a mug of water from the pitcher on the desk. He gulped hard and emptied the mug three times before he was satisfied. Esther was sitting back on her tail, forming a comfortable S-shape, and watched Sir Duffy with quiet interest. He paced in front of her and mumbled to himself.

"Now . . . now, just remember what she told you." He glanced at Esther. "Ride to the Truegone peak with the cave." He stopped and reached into his pocket, pulling out a silver compass on a silver chain. Carved on the outer lid was an ore badger curled around a red stone. He flipped it open, saw the metal arrow pointing to proper north, and nodded. Sir Duffy snapped the compass shut and thumbed the carving. His eyes started to water.

"Right. The boy is old enough to make the trip wif me, but we'll wait eight days. That's 'ow long it'll take 'em to get to Jordstrum. They'll be outta the way there." He nodded sharply and closed the office curtains.

The alchemist went to a heavy trunk in the corner and labored to move it aside. After much straining, he revealed a trapdoor and lifted it open. There was a dark hole beneath. He reached into a nearby drawer and pulled out three clear glass balls and shook them vigorously. Inside, dust kicked up in a cloud and glowed brightly. At the top of the trapdoor was a narrow gutter that sloped downward. Sir Duffy tossed the balls into it. As they rolled down into the hole, the stairs and dirt floor of the cellar lit up.

He took a perfume bottle with an atomizer from the same drawer, and snatched a bag of dead dogflies from a hook. He stepped onto the rickety steps, hearing them creak in protest to his unwelcome weight. The wooden steps held, but Sir Duffy squirmed a little to get his belly through the opening. "I've been eatin' too many cakes," he grumbled.

Sir Duffy had to stoop a little to avoid the overhead support beams. The small room was not the entire cellar but an isolated compartment. In the far corner, a plant was moving. The main body was a thick green stalk and on top rested a bulbous head about the size of a tea kettle. It turned in Sir Duffy's direction and divided its head into four parts, opening into a mouth and flashing rows of sharp teeth with a hiss. Encroaching vine appendages climbed up the walls and curled fist-like in the air around its body. The plant flexed its limbs in a territorial display of aggression.

"You'd fink you'd know me by now and not give me any trouble, you stupid zucchini." Sir Duffy opened the bag and took out a handful of dead dogflies. The gargum plant stopped hissing and raised several shoots with miniature bulbous heads on the ends. He tossed the insects at the creature. All the heads deftly snatched the bugs out of the air. The plant raised its heads in anticipation of more. "No more, you greedy vegetable. I don't want you gettin' too big and takin' one of me 'ands off." He squeezed the atomizer several times, just out of reach of the plant's searching appendages. The mist traveled over the big head, which sniffed at the spray and then shivered. The encroaching vines stopped moving, and all the heads drooped in slumber.

"You 'ave any idea 'ow expensive talking rabbit spit is? Mindless turnip." Sir Duffy knelt down next to the unconscious plant. At the base of the thick stalk were two frying pan-sized leaves. He lifted one and started scraping away fistfuls of dirt. A couple of inches below, he uncovered a square stone with a circle of markings on its surface. The raised letters were from a foreign alphabet, but they didn't spell anything. Sir Duffy cleared away the dirt, blowing on it several times. He thumbed the letters and whispered to himself, "Kepme su cretme . . . keep my secret." He pressed down on five of the letters and the stone lid popped upward. The plant twitched and gave a hiss but continued to sleep. Sir Duffy flipped the lid over, uncovering a stone-lined cubbyhole.

Inside, there was a book and a black silk coin purse. He grabbed the coin purse and untied the bindings. He tipped it, and what fell into his lap made his body go cold. Resting heavily on his legs were two jagged crystals, each about the size of his fist. Putrid's Hearts. The edges were clear, but inside, clouds of red, menacing smoke swirled in agitation. Sir Duffy stared at them, sick with fear. Flashes of horrible memories filled his head and a wave of nausea rippled through him.

He stuck the evil things back into the purse and replaced the bag in the cubbyhole. For a few moments Sir Duffy stared at the wall, his eyes welling with tears. He gave a great sniff, wiped his sweating forehead with the back of his sleeve and blinked away the tears. With the same gentleness he used while handling Esther, he removed the leather-bound book. The cover was very worn and the edges frayed. He flipped it open, and the sight of the first page caused his eyes to blur with emotion once again. In very neat script he read the name of the journal's owner: *Sir Charles Mostly, LAA.*

Sir Duffy blinked hard and let the tears roll down his cheeks. He gave another loud sniff and flipped through the journal until a folded leaf of paper fell out. It was old and browning along the edges. He unfolded it. A new thick wave of tears flooded his eyes as he saw his grandmother's handwriting:

My Dear Henny,

Stop crying, it's not helping the situation. I know revisiting the past is hard on the heart, but reading this letter means trouble is afoot and you need to act with your wits intact. So wipe away the tears and resolve yourself to keep your promise. Remember where I told you to hide the one and whom to give the second. Most importantly, don't forget whom you need to tell. Don't you dare write him a letter! Make the trip. The outdoors will do you good. You are the guardian of this secret, my dear boy. If it happens again it will be even worse than before. I have the utmost confidence in you. You were an exceptional apprentice. I love you deeply. Now stop reading this and get to work.

All my love,
Esther Duffy

Though Sir Duffy was freely sobbing, he managed a snort of laughter at his grandmother's lecturing from the grave. Her warm voice filled his ears, and his heart swelled with a longing to see her again. He gave another great sniff and placed the letter and book back into the cubbyhole. "I'll be back for you and the 'earts when we leave."

The gargum plant's limbs began to stir, so Sir Duffy put the stone lid back and covered it with dirt. He scooped up his things and teetered up the steps.

Upstairs, he splashed some water on his face, hoping the coolness would reduce the puffiness around his eyes; he did not want to make the boy anxious. He looked at his reflection in the mirror above the water basin. The curly tufts of his hair were mostly grey, and a grizzled scruff of facial hair had sprouted overnight. He had inherited broad shoulders and a barrel chest from his father, as well as a round belly. It was his fiftieth year, and he had firmly decided that he was quite content with his constitution, grey hairs and belly notwithstanding.

Esther had been sitting silently in her S-shape, arms folded, watching Sir Duffy. He took notice of her reflection in the mirror and smiled, patting his face dry with his apron. Esther reached out with her arms as Sir Duffy lowered his hand into the crate. She clung to his fingers, her tail still feebly trying to wrap around his pinky. His thumb stroked her head and she purred.

"Would you like to ride 'round in me pocket for a while?" Esther didn't answer, of course, but she didn't protest when he popped her inside his breast pocket. She stuck her head out and gripped the edge of the pocket with her forked fingers. "Ha! Thought you would." He patted her and left the office in search of Mendel, closing the door behind him and locking it securely with the golden key.

Mendel was filling vials with dogfly honey when Sir H. entered the front of the shop. The sweet scent of the nectar filled the room.

"Bring a bit of that 'oney over 'ere. We'll give a spot to Esther." He patted his pocket. Esther sniffed the air and licked her lips.

"Oh, hello Esther! Can I carry her around in my pocket too, Sir H.?" Mendel grabbed a spoon and poured honey on it.

"Absolutely! In fact, it's important that you do. Body contact will create a strong bond." Sir H. dipped a finger into the honey and let Esther lick it off. She held on tightly and wouldn't let him go when he tried to get more honey. He chuckled, "Greedy little fing, aren't you? Go on, Mendel, give 'er some."

Mendel dipped the tip of his pinky into the honey and

35

extended it to the eager creature. The padding on her forked fingers was soft, and her grip was firm. Sir H. lifted Esther and deposited her in Mendel's breast pocket. She purred and reached for the spoonful of honey, and Mendel obligingly gave her the remaining dollop. He looked up at Sir H., grinning with delight. Only then did Mendel notice the leftover emotion on the alchemist's face. He frowned with concern.

"Everything all right Sir H.? What was with the Advanced Disciplines folk? That Pfeifer didn't like me much." He brushed at his leg.

Sir H. looked away from Mendel and busied himself behind the register. "Oh, I'm all right, just me allergies actin' up." He gave another sniff. "And don't trouble yourself wif 'em Advanced Disciplines folk. They're just passin' through. But that reminds me, I fink you're ready to do some travelin' wif me. We need to 'ead down to the Truegone Valley to gather fings like impfire and crystallized sunlight. After that we'll grab the stagecoach from Dukenmire Village up to Menuva. I fink it's time Sir Brandiheart put a face to your name, and that you got a look at the campus since we'll be movin' up there in less than a year. And depended on time and circumstance, we might 'ead up to the Blackened Ash Mountains, too."

Mendel stopped breathing. His hand involuntarily clenched his chest. "Whadda what?" he stuttered.

Sir H. chuckled. "You 'eard me right, boy. I'll 'ave Tilly Wizum mind the shop. But . . ." He paused awkwardly. "Should I talk to your father?"

Mendel's eyes went wide in alarm. "No, no Sir H. Let's have your friend Tilly take care of it. She's good with him." Tilly Wizum checked on Mendel every evening. She would pick up the house, collecting empty ale bottles. Sometimes she left a meat pie to eat. Mendel's father was usually passed out and didn't seem to take notice of the tidiness of the house or the appearance of a half eaten pie in the afternoons when he woke up.

"Good finking," said Sir H. "'Ow 'bout you finish up what you're doin' there and 'ead off for the evenin'?"

"Sure thing, Sir H. I'll be in early tomorrow, then. Help you with setting up."

Mendel cleared away the dogfly honey and stacked the filled vials. He hung up his apron and left through the front, hearing Sir Duffy let out a long sigh as the door slowly closed behind him.

The Truegone Valley

Sir Duffy sorted through his belongings again to make sure he had everything for the trip. Field kit, check. This large, wooden box opened into multi-tiered shelving, and he rummaged through its compartments, sorting through vials, bottles, tools, and instruments. He topped off a bottle filled with a dark viscous liquid. Satisfied, he closed up the kit and locked it. Travel pack, check. His pack held clothing, nonperishable food, cookware, a water sack, sleeping blankets and his journal. Hidden in the inner breast pocket of his brown leather jacket were Sir Mostly's journal and the silk purse containing the two Putrid's Hearts. He repeatedly patted himself to make sure nothing was missing. Secret artifacts, check.

The alchemist left the pile of belongings and walked out to the small red barn in the backyard. He spotted the furry tail of a weasel disappearing into his garden.

"Oi! Gooder! You lazy excuse for an 'orse. What use is 'aving an 'orse if 'e doesn't 'unt and kill weasels?" Sir Duffy marched into the barn and found his horse Gooder with his head buried in a barrel of bone meal.

This particular carnivorous horse was not the most impressive stud. He was short and dumpy, with a belly that protruded from his sides, and white matted fur that clumped around his rump and withers. The talons on his four-digit forelegs were dull and cracked, while his back hooves were chipped and peeling. His long, scaly tail dragged behind him like a dead animal, and the single horn on his forehead was a mere twisted lump.

"Get your gob out of that barrel, you overstuffed cow. You wanna chew on some bones go and chew on 'em garden weasels." Sir Duffy grabbed Gooder by the halter and pulled the reluctant animal from the barn. The horse stood in the yard ruminating on bone meal while Sir Duffy strapped the field kit and pack to his back. Gooder quietly whickered, lowered his head and shut his golden eyes.

"Oh no you don't," snapped Sir Duffy. Gooder's head and ears perked up. "Don't you be fallin' asleep now. We've got days and days of travelin' to do."

The horse snorted.

Sir Duffy heard the shuffle of Mendel's feet, looked toward the house and smiled. Standing on his back stoop, the boy wore oversized pants held up with black suspenders and tucked into his boots. A large pack more than half his size lay behind him. Esther was draped around his neck. She had doubled in size over the past eight days, and her tail was now prehensile and capable of its own grip. Ever since Mendel first brought the gusselsnuff home with him, the two were inseparable.

Gooder raised his head and whickered at the boy.

"Hey there, Gooder." Mendel approached, dragging his pack, and scratched the beast's ear. The horse sniffed at Esther. As his nose touched her she bit down on a nostril, and Gooder quickly withdrew his head and snorted.

"Ha! That'll teach ya. 'And me your pack, Mendel. I'll strap it to this sorry excuse for an 'orse's back."

"Is it true Sir H. that female horses kill people and that's why only the males are domesticated?"

"I once spent an entire summer wifin a few leaps of a flock of female 'orses, and not one ever 'urt me." Sir Duffy seemed indignant. "They were grazin' in the Weeping Lands, and there were a few young ones 'bout to lose their baby fangs. As long as I kept me distance they tolerated me, and I was able to collect the discarded teeth." He grunted while tying Mendel's pack to the half-sleeping horse. "Can you blame 'em if they maim or kill someone who is tryin' to clip their wings and strap 'em to a carriage on the ground? Males don't 'ave wings, so they don't know what it is to fly."

"Has anyone ever flown on the back of a female?"

"Not as far as I know. I'm not sure one could take off with the extra weight."

"Well, maybe if the person was small enough."

Sir Duffy chuckled. "Maybe." He shielded his eyes and looked for the sun. "We better get a move on. It's gonna take us three days to get to the peak in Truegone Valley."

They set off down the main road of the village and out toward the south, dragging a meandering Gooder behind them. Spring welcomed them. The sky was clear, the sun was warm and the land was emerald green. The morning fog had lifted, and as they entered the forest at the edge of town, the tree canopy dripped dew onto their heads. The Abylant Creek followed the main road, giving travelers water and small fish. Today it ran strong from the winter melt.

This particular forest was populated by a single species of tree called roughlett, named for their gnarled bark and misshapen trunks. The canopy was thin and light grey. Blue-leaved vines crept up the the roughletts, and below them, ashy-colored bushes sprouted dusty-white flowers.

Mendel asked Sir Duffy to name every plant he didn't know, and he scribbled fervently in the air as they walked. He also questioned Sir Duffy about the academy's alchemy campus.

"What will I do my first year, Sir H.? And where will I live?" Propped on his shoulder, Esther watched the foreign land go by, her tail hooked around the boy's ear.

"There's a dormitory for students. You'll 'ave to share a room, I'm afraid. And you'll start wif a couple rudimentary classes, like *Identifying Your Reagents* wif Sir Katie Klassman, and *Basic Mathematics of Alchemy* wif Sir Deckman Dire. And you'll be spendin' many hours in the dirt of the dome, of course."

The boy drew symbols in the air as he listened. "Is the dome really as big as you say it is?" he asked.

"Wait and see, my boy. Only your eyes can tell you 'ow big it is." Sir Duffy chuckled.

They passed through the town of Knothing and crossed an old bridge into a denser forest. The trees here all had straight, thick trunks and grew in well-organized patterns. Different bark designs distinguished one species from another. One kind had green and yellow scales, while another had a mosaic of blue hues. All of them had shiny leaves that looked like glass and refracted spots of light all over the forest. The underbrush was even more lively with hues of gold, red and green bursting from bushes and creeping up trunks.

After hearing his stomach growl, Sir Duffy took stock of his traveling party. Mendel's face was flushed, and Gooder was jerking on the lead. The alchemist called for a break. He led them down a short path to a small thicket to the side of the road. The horse briefly drank from the creek and then dozed off under a tree. Mendel unwrapped Esther from around his neck and fed her meatyweed mash from a small jar. Sir Duffy sat in a ray of light that broke through the canopy. He and the boy ate handfuls of dried fruit and nuts from a bag.

They sat quietly for a short while. Bird songs reverberated through the heavily wooded forest, and a distant chiming sounded from deep within. Sir Duffy was starting to doze when shadows passed over his face. He looked up in alarm but smiled at what he saw.

"Mendel! Quick! Look up!"

The boy looked to the canopy. His eyes widened when he saw the flock of horses flying above. Gooder whinnied at the females as they flew by without noticing him. Sir Duffy chuckled as the horse moved directly underneath the opening in the canopy and continue to whinny at the wild horses.

"What are they doing here, Sir H.? I didn't know they flew this close to Abylant. Why haven't I seen them before?" The boy hopped from foot to foot and frantically traced symbols in the air.

"I reckon this flock is leavin' the midlands and 'eadin' to the coast. It's ruby oyster season. Musta been a trade wind that brought 'em this close to town. Most of the flocks will be 'eadin' north toward the Blackened Ash Mountains soon."

The flock quickly vanished, and Gooder snorted, stomping his front talons on the ground. Sir Duffy grabbed his lead and pulled him back toward the road.

"Come on, you wanton bachelor. Time to get a move on."

They continued on, with Gooder moving a little faster. Esther sniffed the unfamiliar, wild air from her perch on Mendel's shoulder.

"Is there anything dangerous living in the valley, Sir H.?" asked Mendel.

"Well nofin' you need to worry 'bout. Though, we are goin' to 'ave to deal wif one of the largest gargem thatches that I've ever seen. The talking rabbits of the valley call this particular gargem Wek. Its body is as tall as me and some of its smaller 'eads are your size." Sir Duffy thought of the gargem living below his office and felt grateful that it wasn't very big.

"Whoa . . . what are we going to do about the thatch then?" asked Mendel.

"Tell you the truth, I'm not quite sure yet. But don't you worry, we'll figure it out. We've got options."

"Will we find impfire and crystallized sunlight at the thatch?"

Sir Duffy hesitated for a moment. He hadn't told the boy anything about the hearts or his plans to hide one behind the thatch. "The impfire will be at the base of the Truegone peak on the other side of the valley, and we'll 'ave to look for nymph spider webs at night to find the crystals. As for old Wek, there's a small cave behind 'im that's a good spot to put somefin' that needs protectin'."

"Protecting? What do we need to protect, Sir H.?"

43

"Oh, nofin' you need worry 'bout right now, my boy." Sir Duffy paused and waited to see if the boy would persist, but all he did was draw shapes in the air. The alchemist appreciated his silence, and took it as a sign that he understood the nature of secrets. They aren't something to pry at but instead to wait for.

Toward the evening, Gooder started to protest again. Sir Duffy spent several minutes pulling on the stubborn horse's halter until it was no use.

"All right, you lump of meat! We'll camp 'ere for the night." Sir Duffy led them off the road and into a small clearing. He took the packs and kit off Gooder's back and let him wander over to the creek.

"Is Gooder going to catch some fish?" Mendel always enjoyed watching the horse hunt.

"Ha! That lazy mule will *try* to catch fish. But once 'e realizes they aren't gonna just jump into 'is mouth, then 'e'll probably go dig up grubs."

Using the tip of his scaly tail as a lure, Gooder did manage to catch two small fish with a swipe of his front talons. He swallowed them whole, then walked to an old fallen tree and dug below it. Sir Duffy and Mendel caught half a dozen fish and cooked them in a pan over a fire along with some hen's eggs and wild mushrooms. Esther was inside Mendel's shirt with her head poking out from the collar. She nibbled on a fish eyeball.

They finished eating just as the sun disappeared over the horizon. After spreading out their sleeping blankets, Mendel asked, "Sir H., can I please hear one of the adventure stories of Sir Charles Mostly?"

The evenings of early spring were still quite cool, so they

both bundled themselves in layers of blankets near the quietly smoldering fire. Sir Duffy lay on his back with his hands behind his head. He thought for a moment, deciding which story to tell. There wasn't much moonlight, but plenty of starlight. The sky glittered spectacularly through breaches in the leaves and branches. A gentle breeze moved the branch directly above him for a moment and revealed the brightest and biggest star of the sky, the Guiding Light. The brilliant sight struck him, and a powerful story came to mind.

"I'll tell you 'bout Sir Mostly's greatest adventure at sea, but I 'ave to start wif our civilization's beloved origin story, because our story is what drove the great alchemist to set sail." Sir Duffy heard Mendel move closer. He waited until the boy settled before beginning.

"Our ancestors lived on a faraway continent, too many years ago to count. It was a land different from Terra Copia and 'ad less variety in its plant and animal life. It was also shrinkin'. Every year more coast was swallowed by the sea. The water took over dry land in great leaps and devastatin' bounds. Our ancestors moved farther and farther inland for many genera- tions til there was a 'ighly concentrated population occupyin' what little remained. They weren't great sailors, but 'ad some ship technology. So the decision was made to build a fleet of ships usin' the last of the woodlands so as to set sail in search of new land. By the time the ships were finished, 'alf the remaining land and 'alf the remaining population 'ad been taken by the sea. With no knowledge of any other existin' land, only 'ope, our ancestors set sail wif a fleet of twenty ships.

"But since they weren't skilled at long distance sailin', ships were lost one-by-one until only 'alf the fleet remained. They

45

were runnin' out of food, water and 'ope when they encountered a ship far grander and more advanced than any of their ships. A species of 'umans called the Primortals intercepted the strugglin' people and offered their 'elp."

"My ancestors?" interrupted Mendel.

Sir Duffy chuckled. "Yes, my boy. The great Primortals. A species advanced beyond our understandin', or so it was said." He cleared his throat and regarded the stars for a moment before he continued.

"The chief Primore told our survivin' ancestors their ships wouldn't make the voyage to 'er 'omeland, but that there was a continent called Terra Copia that she could 'elp 'em find by following the Guiding Light. The rest of the journey wasn't easy, but wif the 'elp of the Primortals they made it to the shores of Terra Copia wifout the loss of any more lives. What's more, several Primores selflessly volunteered to stay behind, never to return to their 'omeland, and 'elp our ancestors survive the wild new world.

"Now, these events 'appened so long ago that many people no longer believe them to be true. To most, the thought of an advanced species of 'umans and far away lands are preposterous, but the people of the Living Arts Academy know better, because our beloved institution was founded by a direct descendent of the Primores that had stayed behind, Molly McMorag. Many generations of students wanted nofin' more than to seek out whatever there is beyond Terra Copia. Sir Mostly's was the fourth expedition to set out, and the first to return from the great peril of the sea.

"'E whisked me grandma away to sea wif a small crew of brave sailors on a swift ship. They sailed far and away until

Terra Copia was nowhere in sight, not that they bothered to look back and see." Sir Duffy gave a hearty laugh. "What brave fools they were. Sir Mostly 'ad it in 'is 'ead that if they became lost at sea the Primortals would show up and save 'em." He snorted. "But they never came across another ship of any kind, or even the smallest strip of land. And lost they did get, but me grandma said they were never worried. All they needed was a clear night and the Guiding Light to find their way 'ome, which they did. 'Owever, their trip was not wifout discovery! For there was a curious sea creature that followed 'em for days. A friendly but shy beast, wif great wing-like fins and a long neck. It eventually let me grandma pet its nose. She found some leech creatures under its fin and kindly removed 'em, for which the beast seemed rather grateful. It did flips in the air!" Sir Duffy heard a soft giggle. "Sir Mostly and me grandma collected and studied the strange leeches, but they all died and withered in the sun before they could determine any useful properties."

"Because everything has some property that can be put to good use," interjected Mendel.

"Right you are, Mendel! Sir Mostly's number one catechism of alchemy."

"Did you go with them to the sea, Sir H.?"

Sir Duffy snorted. "No, not that trip. Thank goodness."

"Why not?"

"Well, when I left the Northern Forests wif me grandma I was ten, which isn't old enough to enroll. Me grandma 'ad been asked by the academy to come and share 'er Foresters alchemy wif the campus. They didn't know she was bringin' me, but they put me to work in the gardens and me grandma 'elped me study for the entrance exams. Sir Mostly 'ad been travelin' the first year we were there. When 'e came back, 'im and me grandma got on straight away. She started goin' on trips wif 'im, but since I was too young I couldn't always go. Once I enrolled, Sir Mostly became me mentor and I got to go on many other adventures."

"What was it like studying with the world's greatest alchemist, Sir H.?"

"Well since 'im and Grandma Esther were always together, I got to train wif *two* of Terra Copia's greatest alchemists." Sir Duffy felt his eyes well up.

"Wait . . . " said Mendel. "Since both of Terra Copia's greatest alchemists are gone, does that make you the greatest alchemist?"

Sir Duffy couldn't help laughing. "Far from it, my boy. I'm no amateur, mind you."

"Who would you say is the greatest living alchemist then?"

He thought for a long moment. "That's 'ard to say. There are so many talented and 'ard workin' women and men out there. I guess you'd 'ave to measure by greatest accomplishment, and I'd say Charles' sacrifice still makes 'im the greatest. No one 'as matched or exceeded it since." The thought of Sir Mostly's death made him frown.

"Why did Sir Mostly have to die, Sir H.?"

He sighed deeply. "Me grandma told me 'bout 'is death. She said she begged 'im not to go. She even tried to go 'erself, but 'e begged 'er more. 'E said there was me to look after, the lovely man." Sir Duffy sniffed. "Going down into the Black Burn Abyss was the only way to get the creature to return to the core of the planet, but as the creature climbed into the volcano the entire top half of the mountain collapsed, so Charles was trapped in there wif the beast. I don't care to fink about what 'appened down there." The thought made him feel cold, as if the fire went out. "'E sacrificed 'imself to save us all."

They lay respectfully quiet for a moment. Small cracks and hisses from the low-burning fire filled the silence of the calm night air. Sir Duffy listened to the subtle changes in Mendel's breath until he knew the boy had fallen asleep. He looked over his shoulder and saw the pale face half-covered by the blankets. Esther had tucked her head under his chin. He took out a miniature light globe from one of his pockets and gently shook it.

In the dim light he opened up Sir Charles Mostly's journal and flipped through the pages. The book was filled with equations, sketches of plants and animals, and many lists and journal entries. He read through a series of pages that accounted for a trip Mostly and his grandmother had taken together through the Truegone Valley. He read over a page about talking rabbits and their crude language, as well as the sleep-inducing properties of their spit. On the next page he saw a sketch of his grandmother using a mortar and pestle. Sir Duffy's eyes watered and his bottom lip quivered. The light globe faded. He gave a great sniff and put the journal away. Then he let himself drift to sleep under the glittering night sky.

Gooder's snaky tail woke Sir Duffy up at first light. His prehensile appendage was digging around in Sir Duffy's pockets for the key to his field kit, which usually contained bone meal.

"Oi! Leave off you thievin' goat!" For a moment he panicked, but he felt the two stones and journal still in his inner pocket. Sir Duffy saw feathers sticking out of Gooder's mouth.

"Looks like you caught a bird, Gooder. It musta thought your 'ead was a lumpy tree branch and a good place to rest." He chuckled and pushed away Gooder's head, then groaned as he sat upright. The horse snorted at him and wandered away.

Mendel was sitting up patting his body with a worried look, but relaxed when Esther popped her head out from the end of his sleeve. He let her snake up to his neck and wrap herself securely around him.

They dined on sweet, soggy pieces of fruit, spiced oat sticks and cured ham cubes before cleaning up the campsite, packing up Gooder and continuing their journey to the valley. Just ahead, Abylant Creek joined a small river called Silent Glass Slew. It was quiet, lazy, and meandered in an elderly manner. They followed the river which parted from the road and fed into the Truegone valley. The valley was on the other side of the treeline ahead of them.

Gooder fussed and protested as they left the forest and crossed a field thick with burrs that tangled in his already matted hair. At the edge of the field, much winded, they stood above a blooming rainbow forest that the Silent Glass Slew disappeared into. It was well into morning, and great white puffy clouds floated soundlessly through the sky. Bright rays of light peeked through the billows of white and shone brilliantly on the multi-colored canopy and blue bends of slow-moving river. On the other side of the forest, a great dark rock shelf rose up like a fortress wall. There was a path to the top made of ridges and crevasses where the forest had crawled its way up and rooted itself firmly. The trees looked like spiders. Long, dark branches grew into the rock, clinging to the narrow ledges.

"See there, Mendel." Sir Duffy pointed at a sharp peak on the crest. "That peak there is where old Wek lives." The alchemist took out his spyglass and surveyed the valley between them and the rock face. "Yep. We should get to the base before sunset. There should be some impfire growin' from the cracks in the rock. And then tomorrow mornin' we'll 'ike up to old Wek." Sir Duffy still wasn't sure how to handle the dangerous carnivorous plant. But he thought he'd wait to see what resources were at hand once they reached the crest.

Gooder spotted a clear path down the slope that led into the tree line. He took off without waiting for the rest of the party. Sir Duffy shook his head at the horse's burr-covered rump and smiled.

"Come on, then. Let's get a move on. We don't want to fall behind a lazy 'orse, do we?" Mendel went after Gooder with a skip in his step and Esther looped around his arm. The alchemist took one last look over the valley and then made his way down the path in the wake of his companions.

Some deer paths were overgrown while others were well used. The surrounding vegetation glittered with tones of red, orange, purple and green. The trees bent and twisted their trunks and branches as though they were trying to peek at different parts of the forest. When the way was clear, Gooder didn't mind trailblazing, but when the plants became thick and unruly, the horse found an excuse to fall back behind the party. Often Mendel cleared the path of branches, spider webs and encroaching vines, or found alternate routes while Sir H. yelled at Gooder. The boy didn't mind at all, though. He loved using his body. Physical exertion was an easy way for him to keep track of what his limbs were doing. With all the chaos that needed sorting in his head, physical movement was sometimes overlooked, and Mendel would end up making gestures or movements involuntarily. But physical activity required focus and direct commands to his arms and legs. Sir H. had to tell the boy when to stop. Otherwise he would work himself to death.

They had been making their way through the forest for the entire morning when Sir H. had to remind Mendel to take a break. Gooder barely waited for his packs to be taken off before he slumped down under a tree for an afternoon nap. Sir H. mixed up spiced porridge and served it with fried hen's eggs. Mendel was hardly ever aware of how hungry he was until he started eating. He ate the buttery eggs in four quick bites, but managed to enjoy the porridge more slowly. It was slightly sweet and had a sharp peppery bite to it. He complimented Sir H.'s meal with a loud belch, making the alchemist chuckle.

The day was pleasantly warm. Sir H. had dozed off, and quietly snored. Mendel was about to close his eyes, but he felt the call of nature, so he negotiated his way past some quarrelsome lattvetta bushes. After he had finished, he scanned the forest for any collectible reagents. He was about to head back when he heard the snap of a twig from behind the tree next to him. He froze.

He slowly stepped forward and placed his hand on the twisting, bent tree trunk. Even more slowly, he leaned to one side and peered behind it. Startled, he stumbled backward. He was face to face with his own image—a boy who looked just like him, as though he were looking into a mirror. The other Mendel looked back, just as wide-eyed.

Mendel thought he was dreaming. He looked around to see if there was anything else weird going on. Everything seemed real. He took a step toward the strange boy, who took a step back and looked as though he were ready to run away. Mendel experienced a feeling of vertigo and almost fell over, but steadied himself against the tree trunk. He noticed that the strange boy even wore the same clothes as him.

His doppelganger didn't run, but was poised to take off. Mendel thought he should try talking to it.

"Who are you?"

It didn't respond. Esther slithered out from under Mendel's shirt collar and sniffed the air. She started to growl at the replica. The boy wondered if it might be dangerous and took another step backward, but he bumped into something. He almost panicked, but then he heard Sir H.'s chuckle.

The alchemist stood over the boy and examined the replica without the slightest bit of confusion.

"Who is that Sir H.? And why does he look like me?" asked Mendel frantically.

"Well that's a cappamorph. And I'd say it's a young one since it's mimicking you exactly. The older ones are more experienced and can change into unique individuals rather than copies, so their predators are less confused and more afraid."

Mendel had read about cappamorphs but never imagined what it would be like to meet one. "Are they part of the canny class animals? The more intelligent kind we don't eat?"

Sir H. thought a moment. "I don't fink we know enough 'bout their intelligence yet to classify 'em."

The cappamorph appeared less ready to run and more

curious about Mendel. It leaned toward him and examined his extremities. Mendel took a step closer and held out his hand. The creature paused and then slowly touched the tips of his fingers.

Mendel had forgotten to touch his forehead and breath on his finger tips. The structure of his senses collapsed all at once. Every sensation fought for dominance in his mind. Did he taste the air? Was his nose filled with bird songs? Could he feel something soft and silky in his ears? Mendel snapped his eyes shut and reached for Esther. The gusselsnuff licked his knuckles. He started there and quickly, with much practice, rebuilt his senses. Once he put the birds back in his ears, the air back in his nose and the soft silky touch of the cappamorph back in his fingertips, he opened his eyes. The creature was holding his hand.

"Curious little guy. They aren't usually this brave." Sir H. paused. "I wonder if 'e'd let me swab some mucus for a shape changer potion."

"Isn't that a really hard potion to make, Sir H.? And I read it's very painful if it works." Mendel smiled at the cappamorph's touch, but as the creature pulled its hand away, the boy frowned; it left behind a slimy residue. "Yuck. What's this stuff?"

"It's the mucus the follicles produce while tryin' to maintain shape. Don't wipe it off. Let me swab you." Sir H. pulled a vial and swabbing stick from one of his inner pockets and cleaned off Mendel's hand.

"Now, I wonder 'ow we could get it to change back to its normal shape. Then it'd shed the rest of the mucus."

"Why don't we try talking to it?"

"I'm not sure it will understand us," said Sir H.

Mendel thought for a moment. He thought about how after several days of bonding, Esther had started to understand him in simple ways. Then he thought about how well Gooder understood Sir H., especially when they argued. The cappamorph didn't know them and wouldn't know them in any immediate way, but he wondered if communication was simpler between animals.

"Maybe it will understand Esther."

Mendel grabbed Esther from around his neck and held her in front of his face. "Esther. Ask the cappamorph to change for us." He looked from her to the creature and back again. At first she just stared at the boy with her small dark eyes, but then she looked from him to the cappamorph. She slithered down his body and snaked up the tree trunk next to the creature. The gusselsnuff began to coo and purr. At first the creature stood unmoving, watching Esther suspiciously, but her noises seemed to sooth it.

Suddenly, the cappamorph looked like it was melting. Colors and body parts twisted together and disappeared. The creature looked like a blob for a moment but then raised itself upright, no longer a boy. It had changed into a giant, iridescent caterpillar creature. Layers of mucus sloughed off the cappamorph and onto the surrounding foliage. Its skin was clear but sparkled with different specks of color. Small follicles moved in waves across the surface of its skin. Dozens of little feet lined its sides, though it stood upright. Its black orb eyes stared at Esther as she continued to coo.

Sir Duffy crouched down, slowly moved next to the creature and started filling vials with mucus. Mendel held his hand out. The cappamorph regarded the gesture, then several of its little feet shook and smushed together. The jelly-like limbs turned into a single arm just like Mendel's. The creature examined its own and then the boy's, and reached for Mendel's hand. It felt the individual joints in his finger and wrist. The boy giggled.

"It *looks* like my hand, but it feels gooey."

"I can't believe it's being so friendly. Shapeshiftin' is a defense mechanism for 'em, so they can trick predators." Sir H. corked the last of his pocket vials and stowed them away.

The cappamorph spotted Gooder watching from the other side of the bushes and went rigid. Then it ducked down on its belly and scurried away under the forest vegetation. The horse trotted over to the party whickering, but didn't bother to chase the creature.

"Aw! Silly cow." Mendel pouted but still stroked the horse's muzzle. Esther slithered back up the length of the boy's body and burrowed underneath his shirt.

The party set off again through the forest, which became noisier during the late afternoon. A variety of birds fluttered up in the canopy. Flute-like whistling, rhythmic tweets and cheerful chirping reverberated among the trees. Bright colors flashed and darted through the leaves, and elaborate dances took place on bare branches. Gooder kept a sharp watch for any unfortunate low-flying birds that might cross his path. Sir H. scrutinized the various bird droppings crusted on the tree bark. Some samples he passed over but others he scraped into jars.

Mendel tried to focus on a single tune among all of the different birdsongs, but when he looked up there was too much chaos to find a single bird. He tried the exercise a few more times, but eventually the songs faded as the party neared the edge of the forest. Beyond the edge, he could see the dark face of the rock shelf.

They came to a clearing where the river bent away from the rock and continued to the south, following the wall. Sir H. halted his companions and decided they would camp on a patch of grass between the bend of the river and the dark stone. Mendel thought it was a lovely spot and helped unload the packs from Gooder's back. Afterward, he stood at the base of the small mountain looking up. He could see the top of the ridge, but it felt incomprehensibly far away, which made him feel slightly dizzy. The boy took a step back and looked at the rock straight on. He felt somewhat intimidated by how solid this giant edifice was and how the might of all of humanity could not move it. A nibbling sensation on his ear pulled him out of his thoughts. Esther seemed a bit restless.

Sir H. plopped himself down on the grassy knoll and leaned back on his pack. The sun was warm and bright. He closed his eyes. Gooder stood chest-deep in the river and drank water. His scaly tail swam in a snake-ish manner behind him. Mendel agreed with Esther. He wasn't tired and he wanted to explore. He had never left Abylant before and was awed by how quickly the flora and fauna changed as they traveled.

Mendel decided to search for impfire and asked Sir H. how to find it. The alchemist explained where to look and reiterated how to handle the specimens by avoiding direct contact with the skin. Then he started to doze mid-sentence, so the boy headed out with Esther curled around his shoulders. She was searching through his hair, picking at and eating his dandruff.

Mendel giggled intermittently at her tickling.

After skirting some thorny bushes, he found exposed rock face that went on for a good while. Mendel enjoyed searching for small things in big areas. At first he found only smaller cracks filled with moss, but as he moved along, he came across a larger crack with small clusters of bright red filaments growing out of it.

Mendel traced the air in front of him with his pointer finger and saw the properties of impfire form in golden wisps. Esther had wrapped herself around the length of his arm and watched his fingertip closely with curiosity. As the imaginary lines faded, he recognized the numbers and letters that told him impfire would burn skin. He had attached Sir H.'s instructions to this equation and recalled how he was to be very careful handling the plant. He had a glass jar and a pair of forceps in his forager's satchel. Using the forceps, he plucked threads and placed them directly into the jar. Esther slithered back up to his shoulders after sniffing the red rock plant.

While filling his jar, he mentally went over the preparation of a flu fighter remedy. *First, you have to neutralize the defensive acid that burns organic surfaces by soaking two pinchfuls of impfire in a jar of goat's milk for half a day. Then, you dry the threads out in the sun for a whole day. When the remedy is needed, grind threads into a powder, mix with pixie's blood and wings, and seal in capsule. Take one capsule in the morning and one in the evening for three days.* Mendel smiled to himself for getting everything right.

His jar was full and had an even number of specimens, so he screwed the lid on tight, wrapped both the jar and the forceps in a protective cloth and placed them back in his satchel. He was about to head back to the campsite when Esther went rigid. Mendel heard voices and also froze. Esther growled. The voices came from the direction away from the camp. Mendel hesitated for a moment, but his curiosity got the better of him. He stroked Esther's velvety fur to calm her and then moved in the direction of the voices.

Mendel crouched behind some smokey-smelling pete bushes. He gently pulled back a branch and peered through to a clearing. His eyes widened with excitement.

A pair of talking rabbits!

Mendel had never seen talking rabbits before, only the comestible class of smaller rabbits in the woods back home. Though Mendel studied all animals, he was more interested in species belonging to the canny class, like gusselsnuffs and horses. Communicating with intelligent animals thrilled him just as much as potion making.

Esther had snaked through Mendel's hair and parted the mop to either side so she could observe the new creatures, too. The boy traced the equation for talking rabbit spit and its sleep-inducing properties. The imaginary golden lines shone brightly with his excitement.

These rabbits were much larger than the forest ones, about two-thirds his own size. They had tawny coats, and their front legs were actually arms with hands and opposable thumbs. Both rabbits were sitting on their haunches with their arms crossed in front of them. They spoke in syllables similar to the human language.

"Nah, Tem. We nah get Wek by jus us."

"Why nah, Lep? We bes in us tribe."

"Half tribe nah get Wek. Why us and nah em?"

"Tem, if we get Wek, we feed us fam all sumner."

"Nah feed fam if we dead."

Mendel knew they were talking about Wek, but that was about all he understood. Suddenly, he felt Esther look behind him and then sit in her comfortable S-shape. He turned to find Sir H. crouching next to him.

Sir H. motioned for him to stay quiet. The alchemist listened to the rabbits and smiled with understanding. He whispered to Mendel to stay hidden for a moment.

Mendel's stomach fluttered with excitement. Talking to animals was one of his most favorite things to do. He talked to Esther all the time. The idea of talking to animals that talked back made his mind dance circles.

Sir H. stood up and put his hands up in front of him, palms out. The rabbits' long ears went up, and Mendel saw that both were ready to bolt. But Sir H. began to speak.

"Nah nah, me nah wan ill." Sir H. didn't advance any farther and looked down and away from the two startled animals. Mendel saw that both rabbits were still poised to run. Sir H. took another step towards them and said, "Me wan talk Wek." The rabbits looked at each other and slowly sat back on their haunches, ears still raised and eyes darting.

"Wha bout Wek, U man?" said one of the rabbits.

"Me wan put Wek seep, nex morn." Sir Duffy started to raise his eyes in their direction.

"U wan but-but berry?" asked the same rabbit.

"Nah, me wan cave wall, hind ol Wek."

The rabbit that had been talking thought for a moment, looking Sir H. up and down. "Why we elp U man?"

Sir H. smiled and dropped his hands. "Giv sac o spie eggs if you elp us." Mendel knew that Sir H. meant serpent spider eggs. There was a bad fever that spread through talking rabbit tribes sometimes. The fever could be fatal, but the eggs effectively treated it.

The rabbits' ears dropped. The talkative one looked at her silent companion, and they nodded at each other.

"K, U man. Morn nex, we be at ol Wek. Elp you, but you elp us har vest but-but berry an give us sac o spie eggs. Gree gree?"

"Gree gree." Sir H. smiled and nodded at both rabbits and was about to leave when he stopped and said, "Wha you call you?"

The rabbits looked surprised at his question.

"I be Lep," said the rabbit who had been doing all of the talking.

"I be Tem," said the quiet one.

"I be Duf and—" Sir H. turned and motioned to Mendel to come out. The boy shot up and walked forward. "—and this be Del." Mendel waved excitedly while rocking back and forth. The rabbits examined the boy with curiosity and threw each other a silent glance.

"K k. Morn nex," said Lep, and the two rabbits darted away on all fours.

"Are the talking rabbits going to help us with big old Wek tomorrow, Sir H.?" Mendel hopped from foot to foot. He felt electrified by what he had just observed. Esther responded to his mood and slithered energetically up and down the boy's torso.

"They sure are, my boy!" replied Sir H. "Thanks to you." He clapped Mendel's shoulder and shook it affectionately. "I was wonderin' where you 'ad gone to and came lookin'. Wasn't expectin' to see any talkin' rabbits this side of the valley, but you managed to find two that are after ol Wek." He chuckled and patted Mendel on the head.

"I get to see talking rabbits spit fight a gargem thatch!" exclaimed Mendel. He skipped back towards the camp.

They arrived at the river. Gooder stood with his head turned sideways and his back leg lifted, grooming his groin. He ignored his companions. Mendel packed away the jar of impfire in Sir H.'s kit and dug out a snack for Esther from his satchel; she had just about picked his scalp clean. Then he helped Sir H. build a fire so they could make dinner. They toasted wild forest fruit and ate it with chunks of bread and hard cheese.

Mendel asked many questions about talking rabbits and gargem spit fights. Sir H. was unsure what strategy Lep and Tem would want to use. He explained how gargem thatches grew around butter berry bushes in order to bait prey.

"Wek's bushes usually go un-'arvested," he explained. "Butter berries are round, golden fruit filled wif creamy flesh. Butterfigs are just dried butter berries. After they are sprinkled wif cold coast salt, they are left in the midsummer sun for four days. Then they are wrapped in tacky leaves for a week. That keeps 'em soft."

Mendel traced the air and stored the information in his butterfig equation. "Will we get to eat any butter berries, Sir H.? I've never had a fresh one."

"Well the rabbits won't be able to 'arvest and carry the entire batch 'emselves, so I reckon we could fill a sack just for us."

"What's a gargem look like?" asked Mendel.

"'Ere, I'll show you." Sir H. pulled out Sir Mostly's journal and flipped to a page that had a sketch of the creature.

Mendel looked it over. "Whoa!" he exclaimed. He studied the vicious plant and its many heads. Down by a curled tendril he noticed that the sketch was signed by Sir Charles Mostly.

"Sir H., whose journal is this?"

The alchemist hesitated for a moment but then smiled and looked at him. Usually direct eye contact made Mendel uncomfortable, but he was used to Sir H.

"This belonged to Sir Mostly."

"But I thought . . . "

"As far as the rest of the world is concerned, this journal no longer exists."

Mendel nodded, understanding immediately that Sir H. was showing him a secret. He kept such valuable bits of knowledge attached to an equation of gibberish he had made up a long time ago in order to hide his own secrets from *the thought*.

"But how is it here? And why do you have it?"

"Well, there's too much to tell in just one night, but to satisfy your curiosity, Sir Mostly gave it to me grandma, and she gave it to me. Now I'm responsible for keepin' it safe. Not many people know I 'ave this, Mendel, or that it survived *the mistake*. This book 'as secrets, one of which is 'ow to fight off another curse if it were to 'appen again."

"Can the curse happen again?" Mendel felt alarmed.

"I wish I could say no, but I can't. The world is changin'. Our kind 'as been feelin' it for the past few years. Wif Terra Copia's young government and intense fears, anyfin' can 'appen."

Mendel rocked side to side. *The thought* began to stir and crawl its way up his leg. He brushed at it and heard the faint echo of loneliness and despair. Esther became alert and quietly growled at the boy's leg.

Sir H. leaned close to the boy and said "But you've got nofin' to worry 'bout right now. The world is safe and sound beneath the stars tonight." He patted Mendel's shoulder and stroked Esther's cheek. "I won't let anyfin' 'appen to you. I promise. I simply can't do wifout you, son." *The thought* tumbled down Mendel's leg and out of hearing range. He stopped rocking and rested his head on Sir H.'s arm and the alchemist patted the top of his head. Esther wrapped herself around his neck and purred.

Before bed, Sir H. told Mendel a Sir Esther and Sir Mostly adventure story about the deep dark caves of the cold coast, but this time he showed him the notes and sketches in the journal that accounted for the trip. Mendel was fascinated by this highly revered artifact. After the story was over, Sir H. flipped through the book and landed on a curious page in the back. Mendel stopped him from turning to the next.

"What's this, Sir H.? I've never seen this equation before."

"Well, to many, this equation is a myth, but to Sir Mostly, this was sacred. It's called the Alchemist's Theorem. Sir Mostly and many other alchemists were convinced that there is one universal equation that applies to all life in our world. From the smallest bacteria to the 'ighest evolved creatures, that being us." He nudged the boy and smiled. "If this equation is ever finished, we would be able to unlock the secret properties of any livin' fing wifout 'aving to experiment on it. We would 'ave any answer we wanted. The cure for any disease, an antidote to any poison, even the key to peace. What's more, we would know 'ow to proceed as a species, the best way to become better." Mendel enjoyed watching Sir H. talk so excitedly. "This equation 'ere is the closest 'e ever came. Sir Mostly was convinced 'e almost 'ad it, but died before 'e could crack it."

Mendel examined the symbols closely. There were new symbols he didn't understand, but there were some basic ones too. He traced the air and watched the foreign equation come to life in his imagination.

"What's this symbol mean, Sir H.?" He pointed to what looked like an X in the center of a rose.

"That's the Diajob. It represents the interaction of elements wifin the equation." Sir H. closed the book. "But this reading is too 'eavy for right before bed. If you want, when we get to the campus you can ask Sir Lovington about mathematics. She's one of the best." Sir Duffy messed Mendel's hair and announced that it was time to turn in.

Gooder had his rump leaned up against a tree. He swayed back and forth in a scratching motion while groaning. He farted and then lowered his head to sleep. Esther snuggled up in Mendel's shirt. The boy lay in his sleeping blankets and yawned deeply. He was about to close his eyes, but said, "Sir H.?"

"Yes, Mendel?"

"Can we always do this?"

"Do what?"

"Go traveling, have adventures, tell stories? Together, I mean? Even once we start school in Manuva? Can we always do this?"

Sir H. was quiet for a moment before he replied, "Always, Mendel. Wouldn't miss it for the world." The boy smiled and closed his eyes. And the whole camp drifted off to sleep.

A loud *clunk* woke Sir Duffy. Gooder had kicked over the field kit. "You break that box Gooder and I'll send you off to the stagecoach!" The horse massaged the latch with his lips, to no effect, and walked off.

Mendel wasn't in his sleeping blankets, which almost sent Sir Duffy into a panic. Then the boy appeared from the trees covered in dirt with an armful of pink tubers.

"Well you're up early and busyin' away wif breakfast." The alchemist chuckled at the state of the boy.

"I woke up when the sky was starting to change from black to blue and couldn't fall back asleep." Mendel dropped the tubers into the water at the edge of the river and started to wash them. "I was thinking about the rabbits and Wek and how gargems are aggressive but they're also kind of dumb. All their heads can only focus on one enemy at a time. Right, Sir H.?"

"Right you are, my boy." He groaned and grumbled as he untangled himself from the sleeping blankets and got to his feet. "That's definitely an advantage we'll 'ave over this oversized vegetable garden."

The boy laughed.

Sir Duffy joined Mendel in the brook and splashed cold water on his face and hair. A thick grey and silver scruff had sprouted on his face again. A little forest grime and grit had worked its way into the beard, which itched. He searched his pockets and extracted a small vial of clear liquid and scrubbed his face into a good lather. He looked over and watched the boy washing the roots and chuckled at the sight of his filthy arms and face, though his mop of hair was relatively clean from all of Esther's diligence.

"You otta turn some of that attention on yourself." He splashed the boy with water, and once the surprise on Mendel's face subsided, the boy giggled. He finished washing the rest of the tubers and then stripped off his shirts, which Esther didn't like. She had been wrapped around his upper arm.

"I'll take Esther while you wash up." Sir Duffy gently grabbed Esther and let her slide around in his jacket and shirt pockets, though she avoided the pocket with the stones in it. "Gusselsnuffs don't like water. The more oil in their coat the better. Makes 'em slippery and 'ard to catch. The oil also 'as a bitter taste to it, makin' some predators spit 'em out. But, silver monkeys are smart enough to know to wash 'em off before they eat a gusselsnuff." Sir Duffy rinsed his face and patted it dry.

"Don't worry Esther, I won't let anything try to eat you," remarked the half-naked boy. "There aren't any silver monkeys in the Truegone, are there, Sir H.?"

"Not to worry Mendel. They live far west of 'ere. Nofin's gonna 'appen to our Esther." Her head popped out of his jacket sleeve and he stroked her under the chin.

Mendel took off his boots and rolled up his pants and waded into the water, dunking his entire head in the cold stream. Sir Duffy handed him the vial of soap. The boy covered himself in a thick white lather and then dunked himself again. When he finally emerged, his hair was wet and spiky and his skinny frame was slick. He started to shiver in the cool morning air.

Sir Duffy started a fire and prepared the tubers in a pot along with mushrooms and raisins. Once the pot came to a raging boil he cracked in a couple of hen's eggs and let them poach. Mendel dried off and put on a clean shirt from his pack, and then added duck fat from a jar to the tuber soup along with some peppery spice cubes.

After breakfast they cleaned the camp, filled their water skins from the river and packed up Gooder. A zigzag path cut into the rock face all the way to the top. A small forest of spider trees grew along the trail. Some parts of the path were wide and others were narrow. Gooder led the way, and Sir Duffy watched with annoyance how suddenly agile and athletic the lazy horse became. His unmanicured talons gripped rock edges and tree roots with confidence, and his unpolished hooves balanced dexterously on loose stone and slippery moss. He climbed, hopped and leapt his way up the path with exhilarated snorts. Meanwhile, Sir Duffy grunted, groaned and wheezed his way to what he was certain was his death. He worried about the boy, but Mendel moved up the path with as much ease as Gooder. Though his cheeks were flushed and his breath heavy, he looked thrilled and determined.

Once they reached the crest, Sir Duffy felt it best to leave Gooder in a grove of fruit trees, so as not to make Lep and Tem nervous. He unpacked the horse and took their forager satchels, but hid the gear in some rainbow-colored notter bushes.

Sir Duffy led Mendel, with Esther perched on his shoulder, through a well-cleared deer path towards the peak. They passed two actual deer, a dark red female and a brown male with a small rack of black antlers. The two animals seemed to be in a heated discussion, though the humans only heard grunts and glottal noises. The deer paused in their conversation and watched Sir Duffy and Mendel pass, and resumed arguing once the humans showed no interest in their business.

The path rose and dipped along the crest of the small mountain and weaved through groves of short, fat fruit trees covered in dark yellow leaves and small red buds.

"These blossoms smell funny, Sir H. Like sweet vinegar," said Mendel.

"These are sweet and sour trees. They produced yaka fruits that have sweet outer flesh and a sour inner pit."

Mendel traced the information with his pointer finger.

Eventually the alchemist arrived at a thicket of red and gold bushes that separated the path from a clearing. On the other side, Wek's thatch stood rooted at the base of the rock face that formed the peak Sir Duffy had pointed out yesterday.

The alchemist crouched behind the thicket and gestured for Mendel to quietly join him. They both surveyed the thatch. The main gargem head was huge. Its thick, swamp-green stalk was as tall as Sir Duffy and half as wide, and the bulbous head was the size of a milking goat. Its mouth was presently closed, but crooked, sharp teeth stuck out at odd angles.

Numerous heads slightly taller than Mendel surrounded Wek. They all mimicked the swaying movements of the main head with an almost imperceptible delay. Long vines tangled in large mattes between the heads, and they twitched with sensation whenever a breeze came through the thatch. Smaller, less mature heads poked up from beneath the woven vines and moved with less synchronicity then the more grown ones.

The butter berry bushes lay behind the thatch against the dark rock wall that rose to a point several paces above Wek. They were large and wild. It had been a long time since the bushes were harvested. The berries were huge and golden brown, so ripe that some were starting to burst, and yellow cream oozed onto the leafy branches. Sir Duffy looked for the cave, but didn't see it. He began to worry, but then one of the heads drifted to the side and revealed a dark crack just beyond one of the soggy bushes. The opening to the cave seemed rather small, but Sir Duffy decided to worry about that later.

Suddenly the two rabbits appeared silently at their side. They carried a sling made from a large branch with woven reeds tied to it. Sir Duffy exchanged a few brief whispers of strategy with Lep and Tem. They agreed that putting the main head to sleep would put the whole thatch to sleep. Otherwise the rabbits' spit would only put the smaller heads to sleep one at a time. After they all decided on their individual duties, Sir Duffy turned to Mendel.

"Now listen carefully, Mendel. I don't want you getting 'urt, so make sure you do exactly as I say." The boy listened intently. "Whatever you do, do not go into the thatch. You can stand at the edge. If the little ones there were to bite your ankle it would only be a pinch, and there's no venom in a gargem bite." Sir Duffy extracted a thick branch from a tangle of bushes, "You can use this stick to poke at the little 'eads that are wifin reach, that will 'elp confuse Wek a bit, but that's it. You understand?" Mendel nodded while writing his instructions in the air. "Good boy. When me and the rabbits rush in I want you to stand over there." Sir Duffy pointed to the nearest corner of the thatch. Mendel nodded again.

The two rabbits and Sir Duffy took their positions behind the thicket. Then Lep gave a quiet whistle and the three rushed at the giant gargem thatch. Lep and Tem hit Wek with four streams of sleep-inducing spit before the others moved in to shield the main head.

71

Lep and Tem took turns jumping into the thatch to draw the attention of all the heads. As soon as there was an opening the other rabbit jumped in and spit one or two streams at the largest head before the plants turned their attention and went after the intruder. The rabbit leapt out just in time, and in synchronicity the other would jump in and take advantage of the new opening. Back and forth they went while Sir Duffy used a stick to swat away any heads that got too close to the rabbits. He also held a pair of clippers in hand to cut loose anyone who got tangled up in the aggravated vines. His blood was up at the thrill of it all.

Mendel poked at a couple of the tiny heads to help the fight. The larger heads guarding Wek started to sway a little, and responded with a delay. Some tiny heads toward the outer edge were asleep already. Mendel closely watched the real live spit fight and he hopped from foot to foot. Esther had wrapped herself around Mendel's lower leg and growled and swatted at one of the tiny sleeping heads at the edge of the thatch.

Mendel watched Tem, who was closest to him, jump in and spit a stream at big Wek, but suddenly his heart dropped into his stomach. The rabbit didn't see that a medium-sized head wasn't completely asleep and moving for his leg. The head was too far away for the boy to reach with his stick.

Tem gave out a loud yip when the toothy mouth clamped down on his leg. He tried to pry the mouth open, but the teeth were locked into his flesh. Mendel saw the entire thatch turn toward the trapped rabbit. Sir H.'s attention was on Lep who was taking advantage of the wide opening to Wek. Mendel reacted without thinking. He jumped into the thatch and ran to Tem. A larger head had moved in on the struggling rabbit, and its mouth was open, about to take off Tem's head. Mendel swung his stick with all of his strength and knocked it away. The stick broke in half. The head seemed disoriented and snapped at the empty air around it. Tem paused for a moment, surprised he was still alive, and then spit two streams at the plant biting his leg, causing it to pass out.

Mendel helped Tem pry the mouth open and then put an arm around him. Esther poked her upper body out of Mendel's shirt collar and grabbed small fistfuls of the rabbit's hair, in a mimicking attempt to help Mendel drag him. The boy felt pressure on his ankle from an encroaching vine. The head Mendel had knocked away was coming back with the rest of the thatch behind it. The boy dragged the rabbit—who spat at the swaying heads—toward the edge of the thatch.

Sir H. and Lep saw the situation. The alchemist charged in and hit the heads closest to the struggling pair while Lep ran up to the unguarded Wek and spit everything she had at the giant head. Angry vines wrapped around both of the boy's ankles. He fell backward onto the ground hard, knocking the air out of his lungs. Esther slithered down his leg and ripped the vines off with her teeth and little forked fingers. Mendel gasped, got to his feet and continued to drag the injured rabbit clear. Sir H. smacked drowsy heads that had half-open mouths.

By the time Mendel had Tem out of danger, the entire thatch was asleep. Sir H. and Lep ran over to them, everyone panting from the exertion.

"Mendel! Mendel! Are you all right?" Sir Duffy shook the boy by the shoulders.

"I'm all right, Sir H. Only a little one bit my ankle. I barely felt it." Mendel's face was flushed and his hair damp with sweat. Sir Duffy pulled up his pant leg, examined the thin ankle and sighed with relief at finding only little mouth-shaped scratches. "I'm all right, Sir H. Help Tem!" pleaded the boy.

Sir Duffy looked over at Tem. Lep was licking her friend's wounded leg. The alchemist went to the rabbit's side and examined Tem's injury.

"Mendel, go grab my forager satchel from behind the thicket!" directed Sir Duffy. Mendel darted away, tripping over his own feet but managing to stay upright. The alchemist gently brushed the rabbit's hair away to see the extent of the bite wound. The boy quickly appeared back at Sir Duffy's side with the bag.

"Now go 'elp Lep 'arvest the butter berries before the thatch starts to stir." The boy and rabbit acted immediately. Lep brought over their sling and the two waded through the sleeping thatch and over to the bushes where they picked berries with haste.

Sir Duffy looked at the rock face behind Wek and then looked at Tem. "This isn't too bad. Let the blood continue to ooze, so it flushes out the wound. I 'ave to get to that cave before Wek wakes." Tem nodded and winced at the pain. The alchemist searched his pockets, plucked out a bottle of purple liquid and handed it to Tem. "Sip that."

Then Sir Duffy bustled through the thatch, half tripping over tangled vines, past Mendel and Lep as they worked industriously. Once he reached the dark fissure in the wall, he got to his knees and squirmed his way in. His body blocked out all of the light. At one point he almost panicked when he could not move his shoulders forward or backward, but after a quick twisting motion he got loose and continued the rest of the way on his belly. Once the cave widened enough, he reached into his pocket for a small light globe. The tiny glow lit up a long narrow cave.

After a few more slithers on his stomach, he reached a slightly more roomy dead end to the cave. He couldn't stand up, but he could kneel. The light shone on the dark stone walls and cave floor, which was covered in bone dust and small mummified animal corpses. In the far corner of the cave, a large spider about the size of a cat rested upon an intricately spun web. The patterns and design were creative, and woven with an artful eye. She raised her front legs and pincers at the appearance of light and let out a syllabled hiss. The well-prepared alchemist reached into one of his pockets and pulled out a silver disc that he opened. The container held a powder that he blew into the spider's many eyes. The rock spider froze and stayed that way as Sir Duffy slowly reached underneath her and the web, careful not to touch any of the thick threads, and dug a deep hole in the dirt.

When he removed the Putrid's Heart from the silk purse, its red light filled the entire cave. Dark smoke festered inside the crystal. Sir Duffy's stomach turned at the sight, and he quickly buried the horrible thing in the dirt.

Relieved, he was about to exit the cave, but he couldn't fight the impulse to collect some threads from the rock spider's web, which, when boiled with syrup, were good for serious

75

headaches. Sir Duffy took out a small jar and a pair of tweezers from his pocket and snipped off some threads, placing them carefully into the container. His light globe dimmed. He sealed the jar and shuffled around toward the cave entrance. The spider hissed a threatening word or two, which made Sir Duffy squirm out of the cave faster than he had entered.

The alchemist crawled outside into the stirring thatch. Lep and Mendel had the sling basket half full. He returned to Tem's side and found that the wound had stopped bleeding on its own. Sir Duffy cleaned it out with water and then dug into his satchel. He deftly prepared an icy clot poultice and wrapped it around Tem's lower leg, and then pulled out a small brass dish and a number of vials and jars. He worked quickly and precisely, mixing together pinchfuls of powder and drops of oil inside the little dish. He whispered foreign words as he mixed ingredients. When he finished, he had formed an ash-colored dough-like ball. Sir Duffy instructed Tem to chew and swallow the ball. The rabbit did so, making an unpleasant face the entire time.

"Take it easy," instructed Sir Duffy. "Eat lots o' but but berry. Make rest lots." The rabbit nodded. The alchemist saw that Lep and Mendel had finished harvesting. They brought over the sling full of berries. Sir Duffy grabbed a small sack and went into the thatch. It lurched about in an intoxicated manner. He collected butter berries, tucked the sack into his belt, and joined the rest of the group outside the thatch.

"Two U mans nah sa bad," said Lep. "Tank tank."

"Tank tank you Lep and Tem," replied Sir Duffy. He handed them a small box of serpent spider eggs. Lep stuffed it in the sling and helped her friend stand upright. Tem put weight on his leg, wincing in anticipation of pain, but showed delight when there wasn't any. He was able to hop with only a slight limp. He sniffed at the poultice.

Tem shook Sir Duffy's and Mendel's hands, which wasn't a rabbit gesture. "Me full of grate. Tank tank U mans fur savin' me."

The alchemist was about to say goodbye when he heard a noise that took over his attention. A hum came from the direction of the valley that could be felt as well as heard. Sir Duffy walked to the edge of the crest and gazed down. The look of alarm on his face seemed to call the rabbits and Mendel to his side. His body froze and his heart turned to ice. The rest of the party stood just as still as him. For another brief moment Sir Duffy felt his breath leave his chest, and then Mendel asked, "Is that a swarm of pixies headed this way, Sir H.?"

The boy's voice broke his paralyzing fear and brought him to action. "We 'ave to get out of 'ere. Now! Mendel, 'elp Lep carry the sling and I'll 'elp Tem," shouted the alchemist.

Mendel ran to Tem, who was about to pick up his side of the sling, and grabbed it for him. Sir Duffy grabbed Tem under his arm. The group moved quickly away from the disoriented gargem thatch and back along the deer path. The hum was almost deafening and Sir Duffy felt the noise penetrate his bones. The swarm looked like a cloud of dead branches that stormed in and infested the thatch. He hoped the pixies were too distracted with pillaging the butter berry bushes to come after them.

They hadn't gone far when Sir Duffy looked over his shoulder and saw almost a dozen pixies following them. The nasty, spindly creatures flew through the trees, leaping and bounding off tree trunks and branches. They made cackling noises, and barked words of strategy between one another. Sir Duffy mentally calculated how fast his party was moving and the closing gap between them and the pixies. They weren't going to make it.

"Mendel! Get down!" He pushed the boy off the trail and into some bushes, causing him to tumble along with the rabbits' sling. The deer path was wide enough for Sir Duffy and the rabbits to stand in a defensive line between Mendel and the descending pixies.

Sir Duffy picked up a short, thick branch and swung wildly at the flying pests. The rabbits swatted and spit violently, determined to save their harvest. Four pixies buzzed around Sir Duffy's head, dodging his swings, while half a dozen surrounded the rabbits. The pixies were swift and calculating, signaling to each other when to draw attention and when to dodge out of the way. At first the rabbits' soporific spit wasn't hitting any marks, but Lep and Tem had as much skill as the pixies, and finally Tem splashed one of the flying maniacs in the face. The creature didn't lose consciousness but it began to fly upside down, bumping into its comrades. This threw off the pixies' rhythm, and the rabbits were able to hit a second one in the face with a spit stream each. The two affected pixies took each others' arms and began to dance in the air upside down. But the four other pixies immediately abandoned their intoxicated friends and applied a counter attack.

Sir Duffy was sweating a great deal. He hadn't hit a single pixie and seemed to only be delaying the inevitable loss of the butter berries. Eventually he over-swung and fell backwards onto the ground. Two pixies clung to Sir Duffy's branch, which he now used to keep them away from his face. A third clamped onto his leg and the fourth was digging through his pockets, shaking and throwing vials and bottles over its shoulder.

The other pixies had managed to separate Lep and Tem. Lep was up against a tree, swatting furiously at two of the cackling creatures. Sir Duffy heard a loud yip and glanced over to see Lep being bitten on the ear. In that moment of distraction, the pixie on his leg ripped his pants and bit his exposed flesh. He felt a fiery pinch that burned up the length of his shin. The pain made him falter with the branch, and one of the pixies swiped at his face, scratching his cheek. This time the burning went straight to his eye and his vision blurred.

Through his good eye he saw the other pixie about to bite his nose, when it suddenly disappeared. Its companion looked around in confusion when it too disappeared. Sir Duffy brought his good eye about and found Mendel standing over him holding the hefty long stem and roots of a plant. The boy brought the heavy end down on the pixie that was going through the alchemist's pockets. He hit the creature square on the head but also hit Sir Duffy in the stomach, knocking the wind out of him. The pixie on his leg flew over his head and into the bushes before Mendel could muster up another swing. Sir Duffy gasped for breath and then looked at the pixie on his chest. It was stumbling around, trying to get to its feet. Sir Duffy slapped it away with the back of his hand.

The alchemist rolled onto his side and pushed himself up onto his elbow. A wave of dizziness and nausea hit him. He felt the world beneath him spinning, and he held on for dear life so he would not be flung into the sky. There was another yip from the rabbits but Sir Duffy was more concerned with

Mendel. He closed his bad eye, which helped slow down the spinning. With the other eye he found the boy swinging at the pixie that had rebounded out from the bushes.

Mendel grunted as he swung at the flying menace with the might of a twelve year old. He missed it, and the plant's thick stalk came around and hit him in the side of the head, knocking him to the ground. The boy tried to reorient himself, but the pixie flew in his face. Sir Duffy tried to go after the boy, but the other two pixies Mendel had knocked away pounced on him. He protected his face with his arms. They yanked and scraped at the tough leather sleeves.

The alchemist looked over at the boy. The pixie had him by the collar and was about to bite his face with little spiky teeth dripping with green venom, but the boy turned his head, and the gross little mouth bit down on his ear instead. The boy let out a wild screech that made all of the pixies stop and cringe. Sir Duffy took advantage of the moment and flung his attackers off. He rolled onto his stomach and saw the pixie try to bite the boy's neck, but then a quick black shape slithered up the back of the pixie. Esther grabbed it by the pointy stick-like spikes that grew from its head and pulled it backward off of Mendel. She bit into its neck, blood splattering her face. The pixie struggled for a moment, then went limp.

The boy lay curled on his side, holding his ear and rocking. Tears streamed down his cheeks and fear filled his eyes. Sir Duffy yelled, "I'm coming Mendel!" But as he began to crawl on his belly, the two pixies he had slapped away landed on his back, scratching at his jacket. He rolled over, making the pixies dart back up into the air, but immediately they both collapsed their wings and dove straight at his face. Sir Duffy covered his eyes and waited for the impact, but suddenly he heard a ruckus in the bushes behind him.

Gooder leapt out and snatched the two pixies from the air with his mouth and bit down, killing them with a loud, stick-like snap. The horse flung the dead bodies aside, grabbed a third pixie with his front talon and crushed it. Although intoxicated by the rabbit spit, the small swarm of groggy pixies still surrounded Lep and Tem. The rabbits were too poisoned by bites to defend themselves. The horse bounded over Sir Duffy, plucked one of the pixies out of the air with his teeth, another with his talon, and broke their bodies. His nostrils flared with heavy breathing and excitement, and his eyes glowed with hunger. Blood ran from his mouth and dripped from his claws.

The last four pixies had gained back some of their wits. They rebounded off trees and landed on Gooder's head and back. One twisted his ear in its twig-like fingers while the others grabbed fistfuls of his matted hair; they couldn't get past it to his flesh. Gooder whinnied loudly at the discomfort.

Sir Duffy reached Mendel's side and held the boy close to him. He looked over to the rabbits, but they were struggling to stay conscious. Gooder grabbed the pixie on his ear with his free talon and squeezed it to death. The last three were pulling and biting at a matt of the horse's hair. Gooder neighed. Then Sir Duffy saw a quick shadow slither up the horse's leg and snake herself around one of the pixies. Esther tore at the creature's wings. It barked, letting go of Gooder, and tried to reach back to grab Esther, but she sank her teeth into its thin neck and, with one crunch, snapped the pixie's head off. The body fell away to the ground.

81

The last two pixies stopped pulling at Gooder's hair and took off in retreat. Esther snatched one by the ankles and dragged it down, constricting it with her long body. It gasped and then died. The final pixie looked free and clear, but then Gooder plucked it out of the air like low hanging fruit and ate it.

Sir Duffy's head rang like a bell. He heard cracking and snapping noises as Gooder fed on the dead pixies. Blood covered the horse's muzzle and forelegs. The rabbits were slumped over each other against a tree. Mendel sobbed and twitched in Sir Duffy's arms. The boy's ear was dark red and the tiny blood vessels surrounding the bitten area ran dark with venom. The alchemist felt like his eye was going to explode and his leg might fall off.

Esther slithered up to Mendel's shoulder and made worried noises as she licked his burning ear. Sir Duffy searched his pockets for a balm and two potions that would quickly counteract the pixie venom when combined, but the two potions were missing. Then he remembered the pixie that went through his pockets. He frantically checked his inner pocket for the journal and stones; they were still there. His attention snapped to his companions.

He looked about for the two missing vials, but his one good eye couldn't see much. He opened the canister of gem paste and swiftly applied a generous amount to Mendel's ear. Then he treated his own face and leg bites. Almost immediately vision began to return to his injured eye, but the world continued to spin underneath him.

"Oi! Gooder!" The horse raised his head in Sir Duffy's direction, pixie limbs sticking out of the corners of his mouth. "Look 'round for a vial of red!" The horse snorted, stared at the alchemist for the briefest moment and then trotted around the path with his head lowered.

Mendel had stopped sobbing but still twitched, so Sir Duffy patted the boy's head and whispered that he'd be right back. He staggered to his hands and knees and crawled along the path, finding the things the pixie had discarded and placing them back in his pockets. Gooder had collected two items between his lips and dropped them in front of Sir Duffy: the silver compact of stunning powder he had used on the rock spider, and a clear vial of crystallized sunlight. The latter was the second ingredient to the cure, but he needed the deep heart potion to activate the reagent.

He continued to crawl but, suddenly taken by a fit of convulsion, fell down. His eyes watered as his muscles contracted involuntarily, and he felt his saliva begin to froth. Darkness crept in from the corners of his vision, but he shook his head violently and demanded command of his body. His muscles released only slightly, allowing him to roll onto his stomach. He looked again for the deep heart potion, but didn't see it anywhere. Something fell from the air and landed in his hand. Drops of pixie's blood followed it, along with Gooder's overexcited breath. It was the deep heart potion.

Sir Duffy unstoppered the vial with shaky hands and dropped in a few of the sunlight crystals. The potion woke up. It shimmered and shined and turned into the color of sunset. The alchemist took a sip and then another. He focused on his breathing, taking long deep breaths until he felt his muscles relax, his vision clear and the world cease its spinning.

"That's my Gooder!" yelled Sir Duffy. He struggled to his feet.

Mendel had lost consciousness. Esther was crooning and nuzzling his face. Sir Duffy dropped to his knees by the boy's side and lifted his head and shoulders upright. The gusselsnuff held the boy's mouth open as Sir Duffy poured a few sips of the potion into it. He checked his hairline and limbs for more bites, but found none. Mendel's eyes fluttered open and he took a deep breath.

"It was so hot in my head, and I saw funny things that weren't there, like equations in another language."

"That was the venom, but the deep light potion I just gave you is workin' it out of your system." Sir Duffy sniffed and made a noise in the back of his throat. He held the boy close to his chest.

He lifted Mendel and sat him upright on a fallen tree trunk. He made him drink some water while he attended the rabbits. After giving sips of the potion to each rabbit as well as some gem paste, it wasn't long until they regained their faculties.

They inventoried their possessions as well as their wounds. Sir Duffy was relieved that the pixies hadn't gotten a hold of the stones or Sir Mostly's Journal, but his compass was missing. Eventually he found it half buried in dirt. Once he felt put back together he attended to Mendel, testing his eyesight and reflexes. The boy had temporarily lost some of his hearing but it was almost fully restored. The alchemist sat beside Mendel on the tree trunk and sighed.

"What's that noise, Sir H.?"

Sir Duffy was vaguely aware of a dripping sound. He reached behind him and pulled out the sack of butter berries. The alchemist must have landed on them, because now they were a dripping bag of goo. They both laughed.

Mendel and Sir Duffy checked on the rabbits. Lep and Tem were both very tired. Sir Duffy's poultice had come off Tem's leg so he made a new one and encouraged the rabbit to drink some pixies' blood, but the rabbit just looked at him like he was mad.

"You get back okay?" asked Sir Duffy. The rabbits assured them they would make it and said their goodbyes after giving the humans a handful of butter berries to replace their spoiled ones. They all wanted to get moving before any more pixies broke off from the raid. The rabbits hobbled away with their sling of berries and disappeared into the trees.

Sir Duffy and Mendel found their gear and lethargically tied it to Gooder, who was licking blood from his coat. Esther curled around Mendel's neck and fell asleep. Gooder pranced ahead of them down the zigzagged path. They made their way slowly behind him. Sir Duffy felt an ache behind his eyes and had a slight limp. Mendel held onto his ear with one hand while he stroked Esther with the other. They were quiet the whole way down.

By the time they reached the river the sun had disappeared behind the rock shelf. Their camp was in shadow, though it was still late afternoon. Gooder was already halfway into the water, flicking his head in the air and braying. The horse had pulled the packs and kit from his back. Sir Duffy didn't know he could do that. The gear lay in a pile next to the river. The alchemist and the boy sank to the ground, leaned against their packs and immediately dozed off.

When they woke, it was dusk and the sky was a purple-blue color. Feeling somewhat recovered, they cleaned up in the river, refreshing themselves with the cool water. They made a wild strawberry and sour cabbage stew for dinner. After their meal, they ate the fresh butter berries. Esther licked the sweet gooey flesh from Mendel's face and hands. The boy giggled wildly. Sir Duffy thoroughly scratched Gooder behind the ears, grateful that he had saved him from all kinds of misery. Then he grabbed the horse's twisted horn and gently shook his head. Gooder nudged Sir Duffy until the man fell over laughing. The horse threw his head back and curled his upper lip into a smile.

As the last of the light faded, Sir Duffy asked Mendel if he wanted to help look for crystallized sunlight.

"Oh yes!" exclaimed the boy.

"We'll just search 'round the edge of the forest 'ere. We best conserve our energy for the 'ike tomorrow." Sir Duffy rummaged through his supplies and pulled out a pair of soft-tipped tweezers, a small light globe and a jar of milky liquid.

Mendel followed him closely as he searched along the treeline for nymph spider webs. As Sir Duffy explained the alchemical process that created crystallized sunlight, the boy traced the air with his finger.

"Now, the nymph's webbin' kinda sweats, and droplets of moisture form along the threads. During the day, sunlight becomes trapped in the drops." He paused to survey some nearby bushes but found nothing and moved on. "At night they stay lit up, but the light slowly escapes and the drops become dimmer. But if the drops soak in this 'ere jar of gypsum milk then the reaction turns 'em to crystal, capturin' the light inside." Sir Duffy told Mendel the equation for the alchemical reaction, which he neatly traced before him. "And when the crystal mixes wif red chingsa saliva it dissolves, releasin' the alchemical light." He paused again, trying to spot the glittering light of the webs.

"Sir H., why does a nymph's web light up? Doesn't it warn insects to stay away?" asked Mendel.

"Excellent question, my boy! Nymphs feed on certain species of moth that are attracted to light, so the droplets act as a lure." The boy scribbled this into his imaginary notes.

Sir Duffy spotted a shimmering arrangement of light specs between two tree trunks. Mendel hopped from foot to foot with excitement. The alchemist let the boy gently thrum the threads with the felt-tipped tweezers, causing the droplets to fall into the jar of gypsum milk. They had collected a quarter of the drops when a very large nymph spider came quietly crawling across her web. Mendel darted away squealing and Sir Duffy followed him with a yelp of surprise. They ran back to the camp as though spiders were chasing them, laughing at the thrill.

Gooder had lain down by the low-burning fire and whickered at them. They collapsed alongside the horse with laughter and exhaustion. After the crystals had set, Sir Duffy fished them out and let the boy hold them. Mendel touched his forehead twice, breathed on his fingertips and grabbed the specimens. The white jewels shimmered in his hand and lit up his face. Sir Duffy eventually packed them away, and they both arranged their sleeping blankets.

The alchemist looked through Sir Mostly's journal for another story to tell. Mendel took a deep breath and asked, "What were you doing in that cave, Sir H.? I mean . . . am I allowed to know? That was an awful lot of trouble, so we must have been doing something important, right?"

Sir Duffy considered for a moment. He thought about how

brave the boy had been and how he acted quickly when people needed help, even though it had caused Sir Duffy much grief to see him hurt. But he trusted him and felt confident that the boy was capable.

"Mendel, my dear boy, if we talk 'bout this, it will change fings. You won't just be a boy from Abylant. You'll be the guardian of a secret, and obligated to protect that secret. Do you understand me?"

"I don't want to be just a boy from Abylant, Sir H. I want to be like you."

Sir Duffy's heart swelled. "I'm going to show you somefin'." He reached inside his jacket pocket and pulled out the silk coin purse. The boy sat forward. "I can't tell you everyfin', but what I will say is that we know somefin' that the rest of the world doesn't. That cruel beast that caused so much chaos 'ad family, and its kin know that our surface exists. They're searchin' for it. But luckily the tunnel the creature made 'as collapsed and the family 'as been searchin' their old tunnels, none of which lead to us. It was me grandma who discovered the truth 'bout the beasts."

"How did she find out, Sir H.?"

"From the Great Lady. She was a good friend of me grandma's and she's our communities most trusted ally. Protectin' 'er identity is an important part of our quest to preserve Terra Copia. When you meet 'er you'll understand why. Right now, I'm goin' to show you the Great Lady's 'alf of this secret, the other 'alf is now safely 'idden in that cave. 'Old out your 'ands. Bofe of 'em." He tipped the coin purse and the remaining Putrid's Heart fell into Mendel's small hands.

The School of Alchemy

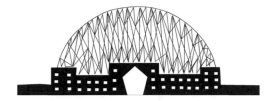

They reached Dukenmire Village in the late afternoon, ahead of schedule. Sir H. caught them a ride on a passing wagon they met on the main road. Though their pixie wounds were healing, they still moved sluggishly, except for Gooder, who followed the wagon with an uncharacteristic energy. Mendel had trouble remembering exactly what happened during the pixie fight, though he vividly recalled the bizarre hallucinations.

The world had turned a hot red, and his equations had written themselves across every surface in bright gold. Then the world went dark, and a foreign equation with strange symbols wrote itself in lines of silver right before his eyes. Time stopped moving, and the symbols hung over him. The boy had no thoughts or feelings about them. They were just there. After that, the equation disappeared and time began moving again. In the back of the wagon he tried to summon the exotic mathematics, but only pieces appeared. He traced what he could into his imagination.

Dukenmire Village was bigger and busier than Abylant.

Visitors crowded the shops and streets in the center of town. It was a hub for the stagecoach in the southeast part of the continent. This was the start of the busy season when travelers from the north passed through on their way to the southern coast.

Sir H. planned on catching the next morning's stagecoach to Manuva, so he booked a room at The Fireproof Inn. They unpacked Gooder and let him clean out a small sack of bone meal. Once his cheeks were full and the bag empty, the alchemist gave the horse a good pat on the neck and let him wander into the stables. The two weary humans went into the pub. The server brought over a joint of roasted meat, a pot of steamed garden vegetables and a bowl of creamed squashes. Mendel ate with his hands. Anything that fell to the table or stuck to his face was gobbled up by the equally hungry Esther. When they finished, the two gentleman sat back, took a deep breath and rubbed their distended bellies.

Mendel started to doze when Sir H. pulled him to his feet and led the way to their room. It held two small beds, a desk and a small table, and a sink with running water, a new technology that hadn't reached Abylant yet. It took a while to get past their awe and curiosity over the free-flowing indoor water. Sir H. whooped and laughed every time Mendel twisted the flower-shaped spout and released the water. They plugged the sink and let it fill to the top, and took turns dunking their heads.

Eventually they took to washing up and scrubbing the dirt out of their clothes. After hanging damp shirts and whatnot in front of the one small window, they collapsed into their beds and fell asleep. Esther coiled up in Mendel's hair, and the room filled with quiet snores.

In the morning, after a meal of spiced oats, sweet fruits, and cheesy eggs, they stood inside the stagecoach station, a large brick stable area with a tall archway and wide turnaround. They waited for the Manuva coach to arrive. Mendel rocked from foot to foot while imagining his visit to the capital and the School of Alchemy. The two of them watched smaller coaches drop off and pick up passengers.

Gooder stuck his head inside the stall of an annoyed horse and licked the salt block. A stable girl approached Mendel and asked to pet Esther. The boy and furry serpent obliged and the girl ran her hand along the length of Esther's body, stopping at the tail and letting it wrap around her finger. She giggled and then went back to mucking out stalls.

Mendel heard the coach approaching. A thunderous clip-clop of hooves came from the other side of the archway. He tried to peer down the lane but Sir H. yanked him back just in time. A stampede of horses barreled through the arch and pulled into the circle. The coach attendant whistled loudly and the horses slowed to a halt, nostrils flaring and talons stomping. The coach rolled to a stop. It was long and made of multiple wooden carriages with sturdy metalwood wheels. The doors opened and the coach attendants helped passengers step off. The ten studs hauling the carriages were different from Gooder. Their coats were black and shiny, their front talons sharp, their back hooves shod and polished, and their slender, silver horns were the same color as their braided manes.

Sir H. handed the packs and kit to a coach attendant on top of the front carriage. Then he yanked Gooder from a barrel of bone meal and dragged him to the back carriage. A narrow ramp had been hooked to the door of the coach reserved for animal boarding. Mendel didn't think it would hold the horse's weight, and Gooder seemed to feel the same way. He dug his hooves and talons into the ground as Sir H. and a coach attendant pushed on his rump. It took the alchemist and four coach attendants to get the stubborn horse into the carriage.

Mendel and Sir H. grabbed their forager satchels and boarded one of the front carriages. They had seats together in the back. Sir H. let Mendel have the window so that he could take in the sights as they traveled.

Once all of the passengers had boarded, the head coach attendant gave another loud whistle, and the stagecoach lurched into motion. Mendel leaned toward the window and watched the village disappear. The country road was rough and the cart often reeled, causing the boy to hit his head on the glass. Nonetheless, he studied the landscape. Tall greyish-lavender ladyheather grew in the fields along the road. The gloomy meadows tricked the eye into believing stormy weather was about, but the skies were clear and sunny. Livestock littered pastures, and fruitful crops stretched for miles at a time. Ancient groves of trees set back from the road shrouded large, old farmhouses.

The coach stopped briefly at small towns along the way to drop off and pick up passengers. In a town called Sydopan, Mendel noticed Sir H. peering over the seat and he looked to see who had taken the alchemist's attention. A woman dressed in grey Advanced Disciplines attire boarded. She took a seat toward the front. Mendel and the alchemist exchanged looks but refrained from speaking.

The ride took most of the day. Mendel didn't realize he had fallen asleep. Sir H. nudged him awake. He rubbed his eyes and looked out the window. The landscape had changed from fields and farmhouses to large brick buildings stacked together in rows.

"Look, Mendel. We're 'ere."

Late evening had come, though the spring sun still hung low in the sky. It took him a moment to realize where he was. The streets they rode through were neatly paved with smooth grey stone, and the sidewalks were laid with pale bricks. Buildings two and three stories high lined the streets, and lamp posts topped with a triplet of light globes lit the way. People on stilts walked from post to post, winding mechanisms that gently shook the globes in anticipation of night. The carriage passed small green parks surrounded by iron fences and well-kept bushes. People dressed in stylish city clothes rather than functional villager clothes crowded the streets.

The stagecoach pulled into a cul-de-sac with a large fountain in the middle decorated with a statue of a pegasus. The Advanced Disciplines agent disembarked right away, without taking notice of Sir H. or Mendel. They filed off the carriage and waited for a coach attendant to bring their packs and the field kit. The back carriage rocked back and forth and emitted perturbed whinnies. One of the attendants unlatched the door, it flew open and Gooder leapt down to the sidewalk, not waiting for the ramp.

As the horse trotted over to Mendel and Sir H., the boy noticed the coach attendants looking rather disgusted as they peered into Gooder's carriage. Mendel wondered what effect pixies had on horse stool. Sir H. hurried them away.

Mendel looked into the windows of bakeries, cafes and book stores, feeling over-stimulated by the sheer volume and luxury

93

of sensations. Too big for the busy sidewalks, Gooder had to walk in the gutter. The boy could feel Esther circling his shoulders. Sometimes she hooked her tail around his ear and leaned outward, trying to grab at or smell the strange people walking by.

They turned a corner, and Mendel halted. The street entered a wide lawn that led up to a massive building made of grey brick and red and yellow stained glass windows. It was four stories high. Animal statues lined the edge of the roof, and sheets of dark choke ivy covered the walls. A giant glass dome rose up behind the building.

"Is that . . . ?"

"Yes, Mendel. That is the Living Arts Academy School of Alchemy." Sir H. put his arm around Mendel and encouraged the boy forward. Gooder trotted ahead of them across the lawn.

As they approached, Mendel traced his finger over and around the campus, trying to sketch the sight in golden strokes so that his imagination would have it for always. At the end of the driveway, a tall archway opened into a courtyard. Rows of surrounding windows overlooked a small garden of exotic plants. A tall and slender tree with silver bark and white feathery leaves stood in the middle of the patch. Tables, chairs, and a small fountain complimented the garden. Gooder drank from the fountain impolitely.

"What kind of tree is that, Sir H.?" asked the boy.

"Well that's a very rare tree called a Silent Willow. Only an 'andful are left. It doesn't make a sound when the wind blows fruw it and the sap will calm the wildest of beasts or the maddest of people."

Another archway stood on the opposite side of the courtyard. As they approached it, they met a small man with dark
skin and grey hair coming through. He was slightly taller than
Mendel and wore a red coat and black pants rolled up to his
knees, revealing bare feet and dirt-covered toes.

"Henny! What a delight! My heart always warms at the
return of our alumni." The man approached with open arms.

"Sir Wattmen! It's been ages." Sir H. embraced the man.

"And who do we have here?" asked Sir Wattmen.

"This is Mendel, me apprentice." Mendel felt Sir H. urge
him forward. "This is Sir Dominic Wattmen, the chancellor of
the School of Alchemy."

Mendel felt nervous meeting the man who would accept
or deny his application to the school next year. Looking at
the gentleman's feet, he extended his hand and waited for it
to be grasped, but suddenly the small man seized him in a
surprisingly strong embrace. Sir Wattmen released Mendel
and examined him with old, brown eyes.

"I must say, the last time a Primore was admitted to this
campus was ten years ago! They are so rare these days. Sir
Lovington was the last, and thank my stars, she is still here,
a teacher now. She will be delighted to meet you. I have been
most excited to receive your application young man. I look forward to reviewing it! And Henny! I am so glad you've finally
accepted a teaching position here."

Mendel had trouble processing what Sir Wattman was saying. Some of it excited him while some of it worried him, but
he couldn't sort the information fast enough. *The thought* began
to whisper from down below, and panic seized him. He was on
the verge of losing his way when Sir H.'s voice cleared his head.

"Mendel is goin' to fit right in 'ere, I reckon. I 'aven't seen such a natural alchemist in all me years. And I'm thrilled to be returning to me old stomping grounds. But we still 'ave plenty of time before we need to worry 'bout applications, and movin' shop and such. All that's on our minds right now is seeing the dome and then gettin' somefing to eat." He patted Mendel on the shoulder reassuringly, and the boy felt *the thought* slip down into the darkness and away from his mind.

"Of course, of course!" exclaimed Sir Wattmen. "You must be famished and exhausted! Please, don't let me keep you. I will inform Johan that you are here. I must wash up for supper myself. Oh, we have running water installed in some of the east rooms. We will be sure to board you there! What a luxury!" Sir Wattmen trotted away and disappeared behind a door.

Mendel took a breath and found Esther's tail. He played with it absently while absorbing and processing his surroundings. They passed through the archway and entered the dome, which enclosed a garden the size of Abylant. Beams, shafts and rays of the setting sunlight shone into the dome at low angles. Some of the dome's glass panes let light straight through, others blocked or refracted it. A few were faintly colored, tinting the light pink, gold and lavender. Patches of trees grew throughout the structure. Some grew short and fat, some grew tall and thin and reached the highest point of the dome. Thick vines crawled up window struts all the way to the dome's apex. Strange pods of blooming flowers floated above their heads. Exotic plant life grew everywhere. A confusion of scents filled the air. Esther turned in circles on the boy's shoulder and sniffed frantically. The full spectrum of colors glowed in the setting sunlight, and Mendel felt he was seeing some colors for the first time in his life.

A number of gravel paths led into the wonderland before them.

"Go 'ead and look 'round, Mendel, but stick to the paths and don't touch anyfin' you don't recognize. There are some dangerous plants in 'ere."

"I'll be careful Sir H., I promise." Mendel dropped his pack and took off down one of the paths with Esther spinning in his hair. Sir H. sat down at a small table to rest. The boy stopped every couple of steps and shouted out descriptions of the foreign plant life. The alchemist responded with names and beneficial properties. Mendel hurried desperately to try and see everything in the dome before the day ended. The thought of not observing the entire biome made his chest tight. His breath quickened as he dashed from exotic lifeform to exotic lifeform. He scribbled in the air fervently, only faintly aware of how sore it made his arm and shoulder. Pain, discomfort and lonely thoughts were impossible for him to feel in this endless world of curiosity.

Sir Duffy dozed off and began to dream about scorched skies, darkness and loss. Instead of being the scared young man during the Dark Days, he was now the rational master of his craft. He felt like he could stop it all, and save Sir Mostly. He heard the man's voice calling his name, and then woke up.

"Henny, my lad!" Sir Brandiheart approached from the courtyard. He was a tall man with brown skin, a big belly and wild white hair.

Sir Duffy got to his feet. "Johan! My dear friend!" They

embraced. He felt unexpected relief to see his friend. "I know you weren't expectin' us til later in the season, Johan."

"Tell you the truth, Henny, I'm not surprised, with everything that's been going on." He gestured for Sir Duffy to sit back down and seated himself.

"Has Clapstone been to see you as well?" asked Sir Duffy.

"No, but his agents have questioned me thoroughly about the hearts. There's been all sorts of talk. I haven't sorted it all out yet. I was trying to decide if there is anything to worry about, but now that you are here I can see that we must take this very seriously."

"I sent 'em to Jordstrum. I 'ope that will buy us some time. I know Joni Bellamue can handle 'em."

"Excellent. Yes, of course. Joni is a wily one, just like our dear Esther." The two men chuckled. Then Sir Brandiheart's expression turned serious again. "But Henny, it's not just the Defensive Science people. I have been receiving reports of a stranger wandering the continent. She's told people she's from the far southwest plains, but no one down there has ever seen or heard of a woman matching her description."

"Well 'ow good's the description?"

"Doesn't need to be that good. All reports describe her as having pure white skin and hair, and pale blue eyes. Always cloaked in strange dark leather. And she's been asking about the hearts."

Sir Duffy found this worrisome. He clutched the second stone to his chest. "Goodness me. To be honest, Johan, I wasn't sure if we need to deliver the other 'eart to the Blackened Ash Mountains. I don't care to go anywhere near that collapsed inferno." His eyes watered slightly. "But I can see now we don't 'ave a choice. The boy will be 'appy to extend our trip, though."

"I agree, you must go. I have a new apprentice, she just started last year. She's from the Blackened Ash region. Though she doesn't care to return, I have persuaded her to guide you to the mountains unnoticed. Felda is her name. Her mother is Capri, chief of Kapathia. They don't get on well, I'm afraid. You know Capri, I think."

"Very well. We was good friends growing up. She spent some time 'ere at the campus, learning animal studies with Peatree. 'Aven't seen 'er in a long while." Sir Duffy felt a wave of nostalgia and smiled.

"Excellent! Felda will get you to her mother and then Capri will get you to the Great Lady so you can hand over the heart. I think we will all rest easier once she has it."

"Thank you, Johan. I need the 'elp. I never met the Great Lady. Only 'eard stories about 'er from me grandma. I'll admit, I've got flutters in me belly." Sir Duffy sighed. "We shouldn't stay 'ere long."

"Stay two nights and prepare for the journey. But then you best be off." Sir Brandiheart clasped Sir Duffy's hand. "Oh, I am sorry you cannot stay longer. It is so good to see you. And! Where is this young man you have been telling me so much about?"

Mendel was sitting on a bench below a tree that quietly chimed, despite the lack of breeze. Esther was nibbling on his ear. The sun had disappeared, but warm colors still filled the sky and the exotic world that surrounded him.

Sir H. called Mendel's name. The boy reluctantly strolled

back down the gravel path. He saw a large man with unruly white hair sitting with Sir H.

"Sir Brandiheart, this is me apprentice, Mendel MacKeenie. Mendel, this is me old friend, Sir Johan Brandiheart."

"So this is the talented young man Henny has been telling me about." The large man rose from his seat and extended his hand to Mendel. The boy shook it while examining his large hairy feet, which were wrapped in worn leather sandals.

"I'm happy to meet you, Sir Brandiheart," he said quietly.

"I am happy as well, my dear lad. The way Henny goes on about you in his letters, I thought he went and had a son." Sir Brandiheart messed the boy's hair and patted Esther on the head. Mendel blushed, and Esther retreated into his shirt.

"Well, I see the boy every day, much as fathers do, I guess," replied Sir H. "Mendel, my lad, it looks like we 'ave to travel up to the Blackened Ash Mountains after all, to do some more 'iding." Sir H. gave an exaggerated wink.

"I understand, Sir H." Mendel felt relieved that they wouldn't be going back to Abylant yet.

"We should probably get us some food, right Mendel?"

His prompt made Mendel realize how hungry he was, and he nodded.

"I told Peatree to cook extra," Sir Brandiheart said. "Come, I will feed you well. Don't worry about your things or that blasted horse. Gooder already found his way to the stables, and the bone meal! I will have your gear moved to an east room. One with a tub for bathing. You are in for a treat, Henny!" Sir Brandiheart gestured for the two travelers to follow him. "And I will introduce you to Felda. She will be dining with us. She's a little grumpy, but a treasure nonetheless."

They followed Sir Brandiheart through the inner courtyard and up a small stone staircase to the third floor of the school. They entered a long hallway with many doors and green vines that grew up the sides and across the ceiling. Sir Brandiheart tugged one of the tendrils. The plant responded by shuddering down the length of the hallway. Light globes tangled throughout the vines began to glow.

Sir Brandiheart stopped at one of the wooden doors. Mendel noticed that the vines grew around it.

"Sir Brandiheart, what kind of wood is the door made of?" he asked. "And how does it repel the vines?"

Sir Brandiheart looked at Sir H. and smiled. "He *is* quick." He turned to the boy. "It's made from Gripsnap trees, which produces an oil that the vines don't much care for."

He opened the door and gestured for them to enter. The room was spacious and had two windows that overlooked the inner courtyard. A large wooden table was set for six, with glowing light globes atop slender silver stems. A fire crackled in the hearth, and a string of tiny light globes decorated the walls. On one of the windowsills sat a fat orange cat. Esther quietly hissed, and Mendel hesitated, unsure if the cat had a taste for gusselsnuffs.

"Not to worry, lad. Felda's cat Butter only eats fine-cooked meals that don't move or fight back." Sir Brandiheart gave a burst of laughter that filled the room. He pulled out two of the chairs. "Please sit. You two are surely tired from your journey. I'll have Peatree bring you some water and wine." He disappeared through a side door.

Mendel sat in the chair next to the window so he could look out over the courtyard. Sir H. sat next to him. The side door opened and a thin, older man with pale skin and slightly hunched shoulders backed into the room. He turned around and carried a tray with pitchers of wine and water to the table.

"So nice to see you again, Henny," wheezed the old man.

"Lovely to see you, Peatree. 'Ow's the back feelin'?"

"Much better. Johan has refined the vertamaladies potion quite a bit since you were last here." He set the pitchers down on the table, poured water for both guests and wine for Sir H. He then took a bottle from his pocket and added a splash of the red elixir to Mendel's water. "Lyla, Sir Lovington that is, said a few drops of gravity potion in water helps Primores with controlling their bodies. Hope you don't mind, Henny."

"Not at all. I've received a good deal of Lyla's advice over the past couple of years. Mendel, this is Sir Brandiheart's 'usband, Master Peatree Bidmore. 'E 'eads up the animal studies department and oversees the stables." Sir H. sipped his wine.

"I'm happy to meet you, Master Peatree." Mendel shook the man's hand while looking at his clogs, and then reached for his water, curious about the effect of the potion.

"Henny has told us about the work you two have done together, young man. Is it true that it was your idea to add jellied seedgum to the rootglue concoction?"

"Only because I remembered Sir H. telling me that jellied seedgum was hard to get off once it was applied to certain surfaces." The boy sipped the water and held it in his mouth for a moment. He faintly tasted fruit, flowers and tree bark. After swallowing a few mouthfuls, he waited for an effect.

"You are training him up well, Henny." Peatree squeezed Sir H.'s shoulder and took the empty tray back through the side door.

Mendel sipped more water. "Is there some kind of flower in this, Sir H.?"

The alchemist took a sip from Mendel's cup. "Aye. If me taste buds are reportin' right, I'd say it's everglass flower. And that's gotta be everglass tree bark I taste as well. I'm impressed you can detect it, Mendel."

There came a loud thump. Butter appeared on one of the chairs. He surveyed the table and hopped up with surprising agility for such a round animal. The cat examined every empty plate. After finding the last plate bare, he sat in the middle of the table and watched the side door. Mendel couldn't help laughing at how much space Butter took up.

Mendel suddenly noticed a change in his body. He felt a little heavier, a little more rooted to the ground and chair. Usually, when his mind was distracted or over-stimulated, he would lose track of what his limbs were doing. They had always felt too light to him, as though they wanted to float away. This caused him to make involuntary gestures that sometimes got him in trouble if he knocked something over or hit a nearby person. But with the extra gravity that pulled at his body now, he didn't have to think about it as much. He drank more water.

Sir Brandiheart came in, making Butter get up and meow. A young girl followed him. She had dark skin and wavy black hair, and wore a long red coat over garden coveralls. Dirt scuffs marked her clothes, but her hands and face were freshly washed. She had wide shoulders, heavy limbs and a solid torso. Her eyes were light green, and surrounded by long black lashes. She had a slight frown on her face.

"This is my apprentice, Felda Lavendish," announced Sir

Brandiheart. "Felda, this is my dear friend Sir Duffy and his apprentice Mendel MacKeenie."

Felda flashed a genuine smile and shook Sir H.'s hand. "Very pleased to meet Sir B.'s former *garden worm*." They both laughed.

She turned to Mendel and extended her hand. Mendel examined her like a specimen. She was older than him, fifteen. He knew he should say something, but held back, nervous. The children in Abylant did all sorts of things to make Mendel miserable, like calling him "crazy kid" and not letting him play with them. He didn't know if all children were like that. And Sir Brandiheart said she was grumpy. Is that another word for mean? Finally, Sir H. chimed in.

"The boy isn't used to other kids. Afraid 'e spends too much time wif old dilly winks like me."

Mendel snapped out of it and shook the girl's hand. Her grasp was firm, he could feel all the potential strength in her arm. She wore muddy boots.

"Have you ever seen green eyes as light as mine, Mendel?" asked Felda.

Mendel looked up, curious. Her eyes were so light they were almost yellow. He usually avoided peoples' eyes, it made him want to hide, but she had managed to get him to look while forgetting the discomfort. Mendel released her hand and traced the air while continuing to study her eyes.

"They are my father's eyes. He died a couple of years ago. He was a very good alchemist and fought the Regula lawmakers."

"Did your father die when you took his eyes?" asked Mendel.

A surprise laugh burst out of her. "No, of course not! It's an expression. I didn't physically take my father's eyes. He gave them to me through his genetics. Do you know about genetics?"

"Oh! Yes." Mendel traced the air quickly, attaching the expression to his Felda equation. "A little, but mostly about plants. Not so much people."

"Well, anyways. My father died from a necrodite infection. A rare and nasty bacteria that eats anything organic." Felda looked angry. She stopped talking and sat down next to Mendel. Butter jumped into her lap. Mendel noticed that Felda smelled like cold wind, dirt and some kind of spice. Esther popped her head out from under the boy's shirt and sniffed around.

"Oh! You have a gusselsnuff!" Her face lit up and she reached for Esther, who sniffed excitedly at her fingertips. Butter pawed at her arm, annoyed it wasn't petting him. "Can I hold her?" asked Felda.

Mendel hesitated, stroking Esther nervously, but the gusselsnuff reached for the girl's outstretched hands. He reluctantly handed her over. Felda put the pup on her shoulder, and Esther immediately snaked into the girl's long hair, making her laugh. Butter swatted at the little black tail, but a stern look from Felda made him stop.

Peatree came in with a large tray of food balanced on each hand. Butter yelled "Finally!" in cat-tongue. Peatree set down the trays and took a seat next to Sir Brandiheart. Felda let out small giggles as Esther foraged through her thick hair. Butter walked over to Sir Brandiheart's unoccupied lap, looking irritated at Felda's lack of attention.

A roasted bird sat in the middle of one tray surrounded by mounds of various mixed and mashed vegetables and a gravy boat. The second tray had chunks of diced fruit and a pile of clear noodles dressed in oil. Master Peatree carved the bird, throwing a wing to Butter who was harassing Sir Brandiheart by pawing his face. Sir H. dished out portions of the vegetables to everyone. They passed around the gravy boat, and Mendel made sure to drown his food in the thick dark sauce. Then he forked the succulent food into his mouth.

He was glad for the gravity water because the sensation of Esther's slithering helped to keep his mind checking in with his body. But now he felt oddly cold and less himself without her, like he was missing a limb.

"Oh, I do miss your cookin', Peatree," said Sir H. with his mouth full.

"He keeps me too well fed. My belly gets bigger every day." Sir Brandiheart laughed loudly and grabbed Peatree's hand, squeezing it affectionately. "But apparently there is more of me to love." His belly shook with more laughter. Peatree leaned over and kissed Sir Brandiheart on the cheek.

"I'm lookin' forward to some mountain food once we reach Blackened Ash. You fink there will be any Blackened deer served for dinner when we visit your 'ome, Felda?" asked Sir H.

Her mouth was full of food, but she answered anyway. "Oh yef. My peofle make the beft roafted deer."

He chuckled. "Wonderful! I 'aven't had Blackened deer in ages."

Sir Brandiheart cleared his throat. "Now Henny, your journey is going to take a bit longer since Felda will be taking you the quiet way. Unfortunately, the quiet way also involves going through the Thornfields." He put a forkful of meat into his mouth, but Butter wedged a paw between his teeth and pulled down his jaw. Sir Brandiheart looked indignant as the cat grabbed the food and dropped it into his lap.

"The Thornfields? 'Ow are we supposed to go through the fields?" asked Sir H.

"There are secret paths my mother and her crew have cleared out," said Felda. "It's very hard to find, but I know where to look." A look of anger flashed across her face when she mentioned her mother.

Mendel kept looking at Felda, feeling slightly annoyed at her hoarding Esther.

"But even after you chop the limbs away, they grow back aggressively. 'Ow does the path stay clear?" Sir H. seemed puzzled. Mendel stopped eating and listened carefully, his finger poised in the air.

"Apparently Capri has discovered a repellent that keeps the thorns from overgrowing," replied Sir Brandiheart.

"My father discovered it!" snapped Felda. "Mother is the only who got the recipe from him before he died."

"Of course! My apologies, my dear," said Sir Brandiheart. "Capri won't tell anyone what the reagents are for fear the Advanced Disciplines people will use it to clear the fields completely. She feels the fields are a great defensive border." Butter was now eating directly from his plate.

"Well, that's good finking on 'er part, but I am awfully curious about what she's usin'."

Felda giggled as Esther nibbled her ear, and seemed to forget being angry. She turned to Mendel "What's this gusselsnuff's name?"

The boy grabbed his cup and started drinking the gravity water, unwilling to answer.

Sir H. smiled and said, "I named 'er Esther, after me grandma."

"Oh how lovely." Felda held Esther to her cheek. "I've been reading Sir Esther Duffy's *Notes on 304 Types of Continental Dirt*. She was a good writer. I laugh a lot when I read her. She's not boring like some of the other books I've had to read." She plucked a piece of roasted bird from her plate and handed it to Esther, then leaned over and draped her around Mendel's neck. The gusselsnuff curled herself around him. He immediately felt warmer and more complete.

"Is Esther always with you, Mendel? Does she sleep with you too?" asked Felda.

"Yes," said Mendel shortly.

"You two must be bonded for life, then! Gusselsnuffs are known for their lifelong bonds with humans."

Mendel quickly traced Felda's statement into his Esther equation. His reading had only told him about how gusselsnuffs interacted with each other, and didn't mention anything about humans. The information relieved his present anxiety of losing his bond with Esther to another. He felt grateful for Felda's knowledge, though he still hadn't made up his mind about the girl.

The three men all chuckled at Mendel's half-closed eyes and drooping head. Sir H. clapped him on the shoulder and shook him gently. "That gravity potion is going to put you to sleep before dessert, my boy."

"Oh, do stay awake for Peatree's sweet bean cakes," said Sir Brandiheart. "There are three different flavors and the blue tea one is my absolute favorite. You all have to try some." Butter stood on the table licking plates clean.

Mendel stayed awake long enough to try the cakes. Then Sir H. led him through a series of hallways to the guest room. The boy was half-conscious and happy to see a soft bed. Peatree stopped by to collect their clothes for washing and said goodnight. Mendel crawled under the covers with Esther nested in his hair. Sir H. sat at a small desk writing in his journal by the glow of a light globe as Mendel drifted to sleep.

It was early morning, and soft spring light filled the gardens with dancing rays. The air was slowly warming up. Mentors and students were scattered throughout the dome, participating in lessons, harvesting berries from floating flower pods, or trying to get their notebooks back from playful octatrees. Sir Duffy heard a yelp as someone was undoubtedly bitten by an unruly plant.

Sir Duffy had sent the boy off to speak with Sir Lovington about mathematics while he sat in the dome waiting for Sir Brandiheart. He patted his breast pocket and felt Sir Mostly's journal and the stone, already knowing that they were there since he had checked moments ago. Touching them gave him small bits of relief among the ever-growing tension. The sound of crunching gravel made the alchemist look up. Sir Brandiheart held two steaming mugs. He placed one in front of Sir Duffy and sat down.

"Steamed spiced cocoa beans drowned in hot sweetened goat's milk. Peatree calls it a la-tay or something," said Sir Brandiheart.

"Smells delightful." Sir Duffy blew on his beverage and took a sip. "Mmmm. Sweet and rich, with a pleasant bite to it."

"Peatree is a culinary genius. I would have starved to death years ago if I'd never met him. I was a stick-like young man, wasting away as Sir Dilia's apprentice when Peatree came along. Now I'm healthy as a cow." The two men laughed as Sir Brandiheart patted his belly. They settled in their chairs and sipped their lattes. After a moment of comfortable silence, Sir Brandiheart pulled a roll of papers from his inner pocket and placed them in the middle of the table.

"I'm guessin' those are the accounts of the pale stranger," said Sir Duffy.

"I'm afraid so." Sir Brandiheart sighed. "This stranger does vex me."

"How so?" asked Sir Duffy.

"Well, her appearance could be easily explained as a malformed birth. A rare condition we have yet to see. But such a rarity would have been noticed by someone while the stranger was growing up. We are only hearing about her now, as an adult. The most vexing question is, where did she come from? We are asking all of the continental communities." Sir Brandiheart unrolled the layers of papers and started to sort through them. "Has anyone from your neck of the woods ever seen this pale condition before, Henny? We've sent inquiries to the region and have spoken with the few Northern Foresters here in Manuva, but so far the answer has been no."

"Sorry, Johan. I understand finkin' she came from isolation, but even though the Northern Foresters are isolated, we are isolated as a community, and we would definitely know if this condition existed amongst us. It does not."

Sir Duffy grabbed a sheet of paper from the pile while Sir Brandiheart sorted them. It was a sketch someone had made

111

of the pale stranger. Sir Duffy looked at the drawing closely. The contrast between the shape of her jaw and the shape of her mouth and nose confused him. "I thought you said the stranger was a woman."

"The reports were mixed at first. At one point we thought there was a man and woman working together, but apparently the stranger has both feminine and masculine features." Sir Brandiheart continued to read through the different documents while Sir Duffy studied the sketch.

The figure in the drawing wore a hood, with long white hair spilling out over her chest. Her nose and mouth were narrow and thin, and her jaw and brow were broad. The skin was fine and white, and the eyes were pale blue, surrounded by thick white lashes.

"I've never seen anyone like 'er." Sir Duffy's stared at the drawing.

"Ah ha! Here it is." Sir Brandiheart handed him a small scrap of paper. A scribble of handwriting on it said, "Pale woman. Pale blue eyes. Asked about stones, but called them by some other name at first. Ki something." The note was signed by Sir Kateleen Lexter. Sir Duffy knew Kateleen, an alchemist who studied inter-fungal relationships on the far southwest coast of the continent.

"That," said Sir Brandiheart, "was the first sighting of the stranger. It's also the only time she referred to the stones by this other name. Kateleen didn't understand the word." He sifted through the papers again and pulled out a map of the continent. "All the other sightings track her from there, through the plains, then up the coast. She hasn't come to the capital, though. The closest she got was Bellsound."

Sir Duffy examined the red dots along the map. "She's 'eaded for the Blackened Ash Mountains."

"Exactly. She is very vexing indeed. She appears out of nowhere, asking about the hearts. And! According to Sir Hassem's encounter with her, she seems to know that they aren't stones but pieces of the creature, which—" Sir Brandiheart's voice dropped, "—very few people actually know. And she's headed straight for where it all happened. That's why it is all important that Felda gets you to the Great Lady unseen. I considered sending an escort with you, but that would just draw attention. Henny, you must avoid this stranger. I don't know why she wants the stones, but I don't care to wager that her intentions are good." Sir Brandiheart sat back in his chair and sighed deeply.

"Maybe I should leave the boy 'ere wif you," said Sir Duffy.

"No, take him. These young ones are a lot smarter than old fools like us. They think quicker. And he is a bright boy. You need him."

Now Sir Duffy was the one to sigh. "I fink you're right. 'E's learning fast, and 'e's a brave little fing. 'E saved me from 'em pixies wifout blinkin' an eye."

"Felda saved me from a syth turtle. I had turned my back on the thing while it ate a dead rat I had thrown it, but the nasty little creature dropped the rat and went for my leg. She hit it over the head with the dead rat." Sir Brandiheart snorted, making Sir Duffy smile.

"They are somefing else, these kids."

The two men sat in a comfortable silence for a short while, listening to the exotic sounds of the garden dome. Then Sir Brandiheart gathered up the papers and put them away.

"I'm sure if we were to go up to the dining room now, Peatree will have a fattening lunch waiting for us." They meandered out of the dome.

Mendel followed Peatree down staircases and hallways toward the Slate Room where they would meet Sir Lovington. The elder gentleman showed a good deal of interest in Esther as they walked.

"Have you started hearing her lower frequency sounds yet?"

Mendel shrugged his shoulders, not wanting to admit his ignorance

"No? Well you will eventually. Gusselsnuffs communicate on a very low frequency level. The louder noises they make are for other species to hear. But your ears and brain are picking up her species' language all the time. Eventually your mind will figure out a way to process it. Then the two of you will communicate more clearly."

The boy scribbled everything Peatree said into his imagination while petting Esther's tail. He was excited to learn her language, and couldn't wait to start hearing it.

"Can you hear her, Peatree?" he asked.

"Oh, just a few things here and there. I had a gusselsnuff years ago, but it's been a long time since my brain needed to process such sounds. It's a little rusty." He smiled at Mendel.

"Do you hear her right now?"

Peatree was quiet for a moment. "She seems annoyed that you bathed this morning. There is nothing for her to eat."

Esther was digging through Mendel's hair. The boy closed his eyes and tried to hear what Peatree heard.

Nothing.

"Trying will do no good, Mendel. Just continue to bond with her and your brain will do the rest."

"What else do you know about gusselsnuffs, Peatree?"

"A great deal, but alas, we have arrived at your meeting place. We shall continue this conversation another time." Peatree opened an old, creaky door and ushered him inside.

"Thank you, Peatree."

"You're welcome, lad."

As Peatree shut the door, Mendel immediately knew why it was called the Slate Room. It was a large, long room and smooth sheets of black slate covered the walls, ceiling and floor. There were no windows, but one giant light globe sat in the middle of the room. The light inside was dimming, but Mendel didn't know how to stir the sand of such a large globe. He saw a chair near it and sat down. He noticed scuffs of white powder on his boots and examined the floor. Equations were written all over it. After some squinting, he could make out more equations on the walls and ceiling.

The creak of the door opening startled him. A tall woman with tan skin and long black hair entered the room. She wore a long red coat over stylish city clothes. There was something unusual about her, and it took a moment for Mendel to process that her whole body shook as though the ground quaked below her feet. Despite that, she managed to walk in shoes with high, pointed heels.

She approached the globe. It sat atop a metalwood stand. Using both hands, she pushed it, making the giant glass orb rotate. The sand kicked up and the entire room brightened.

"There. That's better," said the woman in a shaky voice.

Mendel could see the room more clearly now. Equations in white chalk covered every inch of the walls, floors and ceiling. Wooden stools and ladders were scattered throughout.

"I'm Sir Lyla Lovington. You must be Henny's boy, Mendel." Sir Lovington extended her unsteady hand to Mendel.

"I'm happy to meet you." As he shook her hand and looked at her shiny red shoes, Esther popped out of his sleeve and sniffed the woman's painted fingernails.

"Oh my. What have we here?"

"This is Esther, my gusselsnuff."

"Pleasure." Sir Lovington made an unpleasant face and avoided touching the furry serpent. "Now, what is it you're curious about, young man? I suppose I should explain my condition to you, since that has probably supplanted all other questions."

Mendel nodded and had his pointer finger ready.

"I can tell," she began, "just by the look of you that, like me, you are a Primore. We Primores are alike in that we are different. Not just from everyone else but from each other as well. No two Primores are the same. I shake like this for the same reason you scribble information into your mind with your finger. There is more going on inside our heads than in other peoples' heads, and too much to control all at once. So at a young age we decide what to put our energy towards, and then put up with the rest. I see you've given a great deal of effort to keeping control over your body, which probably makes it hard for you to keep track of memories, hence the scribbling. I let my body shake as it will. Because of that, I have a great deal of control over my thoughts. Neither one of us is right or wrong or better or worse. We just are who we are."

116

She paused and watched Mendel until he finished his notes. Once he was done, she said, "Understand?" And before he could respond she said, "Excellent! Now what do you wish to learn from me?"

Mendel had a number of thoughts overlapping one another. He wanted to know more about Primores and who he was and why he was so different, but the very notion of asking more made *the thought* stir down in the darkness. He tucked those questions away with a brush of his hand and brought his original one to the forefront of his mind. This decisive action quieted *the thought*.

"Well, Sir H. said you'd be able to explain the Alchemist's Theorem to me? Specifically, I wanted to know more about the Diajob." Mendel felt nervous and a bit out of his element. He had been studying alchemical mathematics for two years, but he didn't recognize or understand anything written on the walls.

"Well, that's an awfully loaded question with no easy answer. To tell you the truth, after I tell you what I know you'll probably leave here with more questions than you came in with. But that's how we have managed to do things that haven't been done before—by asking questions." Sir Lovington grabbed one of the few chairs, dragged it over and sat down across from Mendel. Then she immediately stood back up, looked around and dragged her chair across the room. She stopped at a piece of wall near the door, cleared away some equations and started writing with a piece of chalk she had pulled from her pocket.

Mendel wasn't sure what to do, so he continued to sit there while trying to see what she was writing. Esther slithered her way to the top of his head and sat in her S-shape.

Sir Lovington finished writing with an aggressive stroke that broke the chalk. "So that's—" She looked over her shoulder at Mendel. "What do you think you're going to learn over there?" The boy hesitated. "Come now, bring that seat over here and have a look." He dragged his chair over to her. She had written the Alchemist's Theorem on the wall.

"Now, what this equation tells us is that all the different matter that makes up our world can be broken down into the same material, meaning that everything is essentially the same at the most basic level. What causes everything to be so different are the countless variations in combination and interaction that form each individual object or lifeform as a whole. What alchemists have found over the years is these combinations and interactions of matter are predictable because everything has to follow the exact same rules. Unfortunately the equation is incomplete, but once we complete it we will have created a key that will unlock the unknowns of anything that exists."

Mendel thought he understood but wasn't sure. He looked at some symbols in a large set of parentheses. "What do all of these mean?"

"Those are the variables of matter. The actual number of variables is countless, however all the variables behave in ways that can be categorized. Each of those symbols represents one of the eight categories we have determined exist so far." She began clearing another space on the wall.

"Do the categories have names?"

"Yes, but don't get ahead of yourself! You said you want to know more about the Diajob, and right you are. In order to understand anything else in the equation you must first understand the Diajob."

She drew a large version of the Diajob symbol that had much more detail than the one in Sir Mostly's journal. This one had two layers of petals, many of which had new symbols in them. The X in the middle of Sir Mostly's drawing was an eight-point star in her version. Each point connected symbols in the petals. Mendel's pointer finger couldn't keep up with all the new information and locked up in distress.

Without looking at him, Sir Lovington said, "Not to worry, young man. You don't need to understand everything right away. It's actually better to start with just the Clock Theory and let your mind slowly figure out the rest."

Mendel's hand relaxed. "What's the Clock Theory?"

She finished the drawing with a flourish. "Look at the star as hands of a clock and the symbols as the hours, but instead of representing time the symbols represent other things. For instance, look here." She pointed at a line on the star that connected the symbol for speed to a symbol Mendel did not recognize.

"Here is speed and this one here is movement. Without motion there is no speed. And both require an application of energy. Now, what does that tell you?" She stood over Mendel, waiting for him to answer.

The boy didn't like thinking under pressure. He felt his thoughts stall. Sir Lovington must have known because she walked over to the light globe to give it another roll. Mendel looked at the symbols on the rose. He thought about how the globe needed to move in order to make energy; and then something occurred to him.

Sir Lovington was back at the board. "Well?"

Mendel replied, "Well, energy is something that needs to be applied."

"And?"

He hesitated. "How?"

"How what?"

"Where does the decision to apply energy come from? We have to move the light globes in order to make light. And we have to apply our own energy to move ourselves. But there are lots of things that move in the world. What causes energy to be applied in any situation of movement?"

Sir Lovington's eyebrows shot up. "Very good, young man. I wasn't expecting you to get that far that quickly. Henny is doing right by you." She sat down in her chair. Mendel thought all of that shaking would exhaust him and wondered if she felt tired. "The Diajob is used as a philosophical tool. We alchemists meditate on these relationships in order to gain mathematical insights. In the Alchemist's Theorem, the Diajob represents interactions taking place between elements, but one of the things missing from the rest of the equation is what you just described. Where does any decision to interact come from?" She was quiet for a moment, examining Mendel with her dark eyes. "Here, let me show you."

Sir Lovington reached into her pocket and pulled out a small light globe. She hit it against the side of her chair until there was a loud crack. Then she carefully split the glass open, pouring the dust into one half of the broken globe. Mendel leaned forward and examined the handful of light.

"This sand from the Illuminated Desert has grains of magnetic metal, copper and filaments. When they are moved, the copper and metal release bursts of energy that cause the filaments to light up." She pulled out a magnifying glass on a long chain and held it shakily over her even shakier palm.

Mendel looked at the grains through the lens. "It looks like a lightning storm!"

"Beautiful, isn't it?"

He brought the lens closer to his eye and steadied her shaky hand.

"How," she continued, "does anything decide how to interact with anything else?"

The boy sat back in his chair, thoroughly perplexed.

Sir Lovington laughed and put the broken globe into one of her pockets. "I suggest you start meditating on these relationships within the Diajob before you try to understand the Alchemist's Theorem. Try to relax and give your mind the time it needs to understand."

Mendel looked over at the drawing of the Diajob. He thought about how foreign it looked to him, which made him think of another question.

"Sir Lovington. The other day, I was bitten by a pixie—"

"Oh my. That's a very unpleasant experience, I'm told."

"Dreadful," replied Mendel. "There was a moment when the venom made everything go dark, and I saw a funny equation with rather odd symbols."

Sir Lovington raised her eyebrows. "Do you remember the equation?"

"Only parts of it. There is a series of three symbols I remember most clearly."

She handed him the piece of chalk. "Please show me."

Mendel first sketched the symbols on the wall with his finger and then traced the lines with chalk. Sir Lovington stepped forward and examined the symbols quietly. The boy looked around the room to see if the three symbols were written anywhere else. They were not.

Finally Sir Lovington said, "Very strange. The two on the left are completely foreign to me. I would say they were made up if it weren't for the third symbol here." She pointed at the one on the right. To Mendel it looked like an infinity symbol inside an eye.

"What is that symbol?" he asked.

"It's a very old symbol that isn't used anymore. It has to do with the nature of change. The Primortals gave it to us a long time ago. It was replaced by other, more modern symbols." She took out a notebook and sketched all three symbols. "I will do some research and see what I can find. If I come across anything significant I will send word. Otherwise, your mind has enough to do understanding the Diajob."

Mendel nodded.

"So I will leave you to your assignment. I must find my apprentice, Deepti. When your mind has had enough, I suggest heading back to Peatree. I will find you later because I have something to give to you." She headed for the door, walking with uncanny steadiness on her very high heels.

"Thank you for helping me."

"Good luck, young man." Before she left, she turned and said, "When you return next we shall finish our talk about Primores, until then, just focus on being yourself." The door creaked loudly as it shut.

Mendel didn't know what many of the symbols in the rose petals stood for. He tried to think more about the energy storm he saw through the lens, but his thoughts couldn't let go of the foreign equation. Esther was picking at his ear canal. His head began to hurt and the globe was dimming. Instead of continuing to work, he decided he was hungry and went to look for Peatree.

He couldn't remember all of the turns and descents he had taken to get to the Slate Room, but he knew he needed to go up. He found a staircase tucked in a corner several doors down the hall. The boy climbed the steps, but they only went to the second floor, so he wandered the hallway looking for more stairs. He looked through an open doorway and saw two older apprentices peering into a bubbling cauldron with concerned looks. Another room reeked of pungent perfume and made his eyes water. He saw people in masks surrounded by many exotic, colorful flowers. Mendel continued walking while wiping his eyes. The last door in the hallway was closed, but something on the other side thumped it hard. The boy gave it a wide berth.

Finally a second stairwell appeared. Relieved, Mendel ascended the first flight, but froze when he heard a strange noise around the bend. It sounded like stone dragging on stone. He listened, but the noise had stopped, so he slowly crept upwards, hugging the cold brick wall. He wondered if something dangerous had escaped from one of the rooms. The sound came again, this time the dragging was followed by a loud *clap*. He stopped and peeked around the corner. All he saw was an empty landing and a small stained glass window.

He climbed a few more steps but stopped when he felt an odd sensation. After closing his eyes and sorting his senses, he felt a cold breeze coming from the wall. His brain quickly traced the patterns in the bricks and made swift calculations.

Something didn't fit. His eyes lit upon a barely perceptible seam in the wall. The cold breeze came from there. Mendel traced the brick pattern in golden lines and tacked on the symbol for air, then tucked the information away. He placed his hand on the brick, paused a moment and then pushed against it. The wall did not give in the slightest. He continued up to the third floor.

The hallway was dark. He reached for the wall until he felt a vine tendril, which he gently tugged. The plant shivered and the globes lit up. Mendel smiled.

The vine gently wrapped itself around his finger and stroked the pad of his thumb. Mendel thought of the Diajob and the relationships between things. He wondered if there was a symbol for plant life and a symbol for people, and the potential between the two. He gently untangled the tendril from his finger and wandered the hallway until he found the door to Sir Brandiheart and Master Peatree's living quarters.

Inside the dining room he found both husbands and Sir H. sitting at the table laughing and eating. The men greeted the boy and invited him in to eat the delicious lunch Peatree had prepared. He eagerly joined them and told Sir H. all about his meeting with Sir Lovington while he stuffed his face with stew.

The Quiet Way

On the morning of their departure, Sir Duffy stood in the stables with Sir Brandiheart and Peatree, packing up Gooder. The horse had lost his enthusiasm from the previous day and stood half asleep. Peatree's dog Bootsie, a tall dog with a grey wiry coat and white paws, ran in and out of the stables with her nose to the ground and tail wagging.

Sir Brandiheart quietly spoke to Sir Duffy while Peatree combed debris out of Gooder's matted hair.

"I received a report this morning that Clapstone and his people are traveling north with haste. I don't think he took your Jordstrum bait." His large brown eyes were filled with concern. "They don't know about the path through the Thornfields to Kapathia. They'll have to take the long way. Just stay clear of the roads, Henny. Once you hand the stone over to the Great Lady it won't matter if they catch up to you. You won't be breaking the law anymore."

Sir Duffy clutched his inner pocket. "The sooner I get this to the Great Lady, the sooner me nerves can recover."

"And I will rest much easier once I've received word of your safe arrival to Kapathia."

Mendel had been standing by the back entrance watching a flock of chickens roam the open yard, but then meandered to Sir Duffy's side. Esther was coiled on top of the boy's head. Her body had grown longer and wider since they left Abylant. The furry serpent bared her pointy teeth at the dog, but Bootsie just playfully barked at her. Sir Duffy chuckled.

Peatree called Bootsie over, and the dog promptly trotted to his side and sat down. He gestured ever so slightly with his head toward a hook on the wall. The dog barked and then trotted over to the hoof pick. She nosed it off the peg so that it fell onto the ground, picked it up with her jaws and delivered it to Peatree. He scratched the dog behind the ear and she licked his hand. Sir Duffy watched Mendel transcribe their interaction with his pointer finger.

Felda appeared at the stable entrance with the same frown as yesterday on her face. She wore her hair down, a cascade of loose waves. She dressed in worn brown pants and knee-high leather boots and a grey leather jacket. The pack on her back moved around and meowed. Butter's head poked out of the top. The fat cat hissed at Gooder, who snorted back.

Sir Brandiheart and Peatree escorted the small group of travelers into the paddock. They were about to proceed when a shout came from across the field between the dome and the stables. Sir Lovington approached them at a hurried walk, waving something in the air.

"Don't go yet, Henny! I have something for the boy," she yelled from the middle of the field.

They watched as she took exaggerated steps to compensate

for her shaking as well as the sinking of her high heels into the soft soil. She tried to hold up the hem of her stylish city pants to keep them off the damp grass. She finally reached the paddock, huffing and puffing. She took a deep breath, immediately made a face and held her hand over her nose.

"Oh Peatree, these animals do stink."

"People don't smell much better, dear Lyla," retorted Peatree.

She fanned the air in front of her face with a book, then held it out to Mendel. "This is for you. Take it before I suffocate to death."

The boy examined it. The book was leather-bound, and the cover had a detailed three-dimensional design of the Diajob. He flipped through the pages. Sir Duffy looked over his shoulder and saw that it was a blank journal. Mendel's face lit up, and he hugged his new possession tight to his chest.

"I know you have your own mental method of tracking information, but sometimes it helps to have a space to work things out. And this way you archive your meditations for posterity. Many good ideas have been lost to the trenches of memory." She patted Mendel on the shoulder.

"Thank you so much, Sir Lovington. I will treasure it."

"One more thing." She touched the surface of the Diajob design and rotated one layer of rose petals independently of the other layer. "There are endless relationships to consider, young man. I'm sure this makes things more challenging, but it will be fruitful, I promise."

Sir Duffy admired the ingenuity of the design as well as its beauty. The boy seemed hypnotized by the details of the symbols.

"Thank you, Sir Lovington," whispered Mendel.

"Good luck on your journey." She waved at the party as she labored back through the field.

Sir Brandiheart and Peatree escorted the party to a stone archway that cut through a tall hedge at the outer edge of the dome. They all passed under the vine-covered arch and into a green courtyard with stone benches, small fountains, and a brick shed with a thick metalwood door. Sir Brandiheart removed a large iron key from his pocket and unlocked the heavy door. Once the latch lifted, cold air pushed the door ajar. Sir Duffy noted a stale, damp smell. He noticed Mendel tracing the air impatiently.

"What is it, Mendel?"

"I've felt this before. It was coming from a seam in the wall of one of the stairwells."

"Oh, well," interjected Sir Brandiheart, "when that horrid beast occupied the skies, we took to the underground in order to get around. There is an old system of tunnels below the campus and throughout the city. No one uses them anymore, which is why we are sending you lot into them. They will quietly take you just outside the city."

"But I heard someone open and close the entrance on the stairs," replied Mendel.

"Are you sure? I can't imagine who here would be using them." Sir Brandiheart sounded incredulous.

"I know I heard the sound of stone dragging on stone, and when I turned the corner no one was there and I could feel the cold air."

"Do you remember which stairwell?"

The boy thought for a moment. "It's the one by the thumping door."

"Ah, the trampoline workshop. Well, I will have to investigate. Henny, if anything comes of it, I will send word to Capri. For now, you better get a move on. Peatree will escort you outside the city." He pulled the heavy door open with a grunt and revealed empty blackness. "Be careful when you enter. There is a steep slope that will take you down a ways before it evens out. The majority of the way is paved, until you get to the tunnel that connects to Hillock."

Sir Brandiheart pulled two light globes on long wooden stems out of his pocket and handed one each to Sir Duffy and Mendel. Felda had her own light globe on the end of a large metalwood stick. She also had a globe with a pyramid-shaped depression in it that she fitted awkwardly onto the tip of Gooder's misshapen horn. The horse went crossed eyed trying to look at it.

"It was wonderful to see you again, Henny," said Sir Brandiheart. "I do worry about the future, but I worry more about the ones I love. Do take care."

"Not to worry, Johan. We've survived a good deal together and we'll survive whatever's comin'." The two men embraced.

"Felda, my dear girl, use that stealth of yours to get them safely to the mountains. I know going home isn't easy for you, which is why I appreciate you so much more for doing this." Sir Brandiheart hugged his apprentice.

"Anything for you, Sir B. My father would have done the same," she said softly.

Sir Brandiheart turned to Mendel. "And you take care of

Henny. He needs a smart lad like you looking out for him."
They shook hands.

"I'll be back shortly, my love." Peatree kissed Sir Brandiheart
on the cheek and shuffled into the shed.

Bootsie jumped on Sir Brandiheart and licked the air, trying
to reach his face.

"You blasted dog! Peatree never believes me when I tell him
you do this because you always wait until he's not watching."
He pushed the dog off and pointed a finger at her. "Make sure
nothing happens to our precious Peatree down there. Bring
him back by supper. Understand?" The dog snorted and then
trotted through the door and into the darkness with her nose
to the ground.

Felda's pack squirmed and Butter popped his head out. He
examined Gooder's soft rump, leapt out and landed on the
horse's backside with unexpected agility. Gooder looked very
annoyed as the orange tabby kneaded his matted hair. The
horse sneered and flicked his tail at the intruder, but Butter
just playfully swatted it away. Felda and Mendel giggled.

"Come on, you lazy swine!" shouted Sir Duffy. "Ignore the
cat and get a move on."

Felda urged Gooder forward, and they disappeared into
the shed. Sir Duffy stepped forward and felt Mendel's small
hand grasp his. Holding tight, he walked ahead gingerly,
using his light globe to examine his footing. The cobblestone
path dipped sharply down beneath the shed, then leveled out
somewhat as it continued downward. The alchemist and the
boy walked sideways down the dip and then had an easier
time. The click-clack of Gooder's talons and the clip-clop of
his hooves echoed off the walls. The tunnel was about three

people wide and made of blackened bricks. The low ceiling barely let the horse stand fully upright, but he did not seem to mind.

Bootsie zigzagged ahead of them, occasionally stopping to lift her leg and urinate on support beams. Peatree took them through a series of tunnels, turning this way and that, confidently navigating them through the labyrinth. Sir Duffy noticed many loose or missing cobble stones, rotten support beams and crumbling walls.

"Peatree, 'ave there been any collapses down 'ere?"

"No, not in these tunnels," replied Peatree.

"Oh, good."

"The set outside the city have suffered some collapses, though. But Felda knows which tunnels to avoid."

Sir Duffy started to sweat.

The boy followed Peatree closely, watching him communicate with his dog using almost imperceptible gestures. Sir Duffy looked back at Gooder, who had fallen behind, and thought about their own subtle communications. The horse had been signalling with ear flicks and snorts how much he wanted to eat the cat, and the alchemist responded with idle threats using his eyes and facial expressions. Their usual banter, really.

"Peatree, how did you get Bootsie to push that stone back into place just now?" asked Mendel. "You weren't even looking at her."

The elderly gentleman looked surprised. "It's the bond, my boy."

Mendel thought for a moment. "But I've seen you do similar things with animals you just met, like with Esther."

"Decades of observation and study."

The boy was silent.

"What you have to understand about animals," said Peatree, "is that all species share a very simple language. They can all speak it, regardless of how different their own language may be. Animals use this language to ask and answer very simple questions, such as, 'Do you mean any harm?' If you know how to tell an animal you mean them no harm, as well as a few respectful gestures in their own language, then they are usually very willing to engage with you."

The boy was scribbling away with his pointer finger. "How many animal languages do you know? Can you get any animal to do what you want?"

"I have no special power over animals, Mendel. I just know how to communicate with them respectfully. And awareness is key. Awareness of their needs and their fears."

Mendel stopped tracing notes and thought quietly.

Peatree put a hand on his shoulder. "You have plenty of time to learn these things. If you take a class with me next year I will be happy to teach you what I know."

"I would like that very much, Peatree."

Gooder nudged Sir Duffy's hand. The alchemist patted the horse's muzzle and playfully pinched his nostril. He felt a wet snort on his hand in response.

The thick, damp air was beginning to make Sir Duffy dizzy when he finally felt a breeze. Peatree took them down a battered passageway that let in a little outside light through broken boards. The tunnel became unpaved and rutted with old wheel tracks. After a short way, it turned into a ramp that inclined upwards and opened up to the outside. They emerged at the very edge of the city and proceeded along an old broken stagecoach road. Surrounding them were blackened buildings that stood in ruin—lingering destruction from *the mistake*. The abandoned homes pressed close to the road and hid them from view of the city.

They arrived at a giant decrepit water tower that stood next to a spillway littered with winter debris. Small channels carved into the walls of the spillway fed into the city.

"This kind of tower hasn't been used since a few years after *the mistake*," wheezed Peatree. "They were very effective at delivering water to the boroughs to help with the fires. But the Advanced Disciplines water technologies department rendered them obsolete." He led the party into the spillway and moved aside planks of wood leaning against a crumbling wall, and uncovered the entrance to another tunnel. It was dark inside and smelled like moldy water.

"You sure this is safe, Peatree?" Sir Duffy asked.

"Don't worry, Henny. Only little critters live in here, and if they don't run from you then Gooder will eat them, I'm sure."

"Where does it lead?"

"The original tunnel led to the fields beyond the city, in case of flooding. But other tunnels were added. Felda will take you all the way to the forest behind the town of Hillock."

Sir Duffy frowned.

"Not to worry. You'll probably find this to be the easiest leg of your journey." The old man smiled and embraced him. "Do take care. Johan and I are looking forward to your return to the school next year. He hasn't stopped talking about it since you accepted the position."

The alchemist's eyes watered. "I've missed the two of you,

and the campus." He released Peatree. "We'll see you on the flip side of this whole fing."

Peatree hugged Felda and Mendel goodbye and stayed behind with his dog Bootsie by his side, watching as the party shook their globes and disappeared into the tunnel.

It was dry inside, but debris littered the floor. Branches, twigs and dead leaves crunched and snapped under their feet. Once every several steps something would scurry away under the decaying foliage. Gooder deftly caught a who-knows-what every so often. Butter moved to the horse's withers and crawled up the length of his neck so he could sometimes steal a critter out of the annoyed horse's mouth.

Sir Duffy noticed roots growing out of the dusty dirt walls. The sight made him a little nervous about the stability of the tunnel. There were wooden support beams every several paces, but some had cracked in half and fallen. He held his light globe down to examine the state of the floors, tisking at the neglect. His eye caught something shiny, half-covered in dirt. He knelt down on one knee, brushing away the dust to reveal a shard of metal about the size of a letter opener. It looked to have broken off of something larger. One side had elegant designs carved into it while the other side was striated with break patterns. The metal was unknown to the alchemist: dark in color with flecks of sparkling material imbedded in it. Sir Duffy put the strange thing into his pocket.

"Felda, how often is this tunnel used?" asked Sir Duffy.

"Well, Sir B. had forgotten about it. Peatree thought of it last year when they needed to sneak some banned reagents onto the campus. I've only used it as a shortcut to Hillock a few times."

They came to the tunnel's original end. Light spilled into the entrance and a wide field spread out from its mouth. Sir Duffy very much wanted to see the outside again, but Felda led the party into one of two additional tunnels that led away from the sunlight.

"Where does the other tunnel lead, Felda?" asked Sir Duffy.

"Peatree said it leads to the Witchfine cemetery. But I've never gone that way," replied the girl.

The condition of this next tunnel made Sir Duffy even more uncomfortable. Large roots had invaded, forcing everyone to duck their heads and maneuver around them. Gooder used his sharp talons to slash through some of the limbs. The air was stifling, and showers of dirt fell onto their heads. Butter immediately jumped from the horse's back onto Felda's shoulders and ducked into her pack.

"'Ow you doin', Mendel?" Sir Duffy was concerned that the boy might be as anxious as he was.

"Good, Sir H. Esther keeps pushing stray branches away from my face."

After struggling for a couple of hours, Sir Duffy was covered in dirt and sweat. He felt as though he were about to scream, but then noticed a change in the air.

"We're just about there," announced Felda.

Sir Duffy sighed, blowing a cloud of dirt into his eyes. The ground inclined sharply upward. Felda grunted as she shoved planks of wood and tree branches away from an opening above her head, causing light to spill into the tunnel from outside. Mendel and Sir Duffy put their light globes away. Gooder used his powerful hind quarters and propelled himself out of what was basically a hole in the ground. Felda climbed after him. Sir Duffy kept a hand on Mendel's back as they pulled themselves out.

They were surrounded by forest and light. Sir Duffy was too relieved to feel his exhaustion. He surveyed his fellow travelers, chuckling. The children's faces and clothes were smeared with dirt.

"Aren't we a sight?"

Mendel and Felda looked at each other and cracked up. She patted Gooder's rump, raising clouds of dirt. A sneeze came from her pack, and Butter jumped out and onto the ground. His coat was clean, so he wandered away from his dirty companions.

"Once we cross the main road we'll take some deer paths," said Felda. "There's a stream along the way we can clean up in."

The party took a moment to collect themselves and then Felda pressed forward, calling Butter to her side. The fat cat followed her, his big belly swinging side to side. The main road wasn't far and when they reached it Felda signaled for everyone to wait. She watched the road closely. No sign of people in either direction. Sir Duffy noticed a bend in the road to the south that hid any oncoming traffic.

"We should cross quickly," she said.

Butter went first, not waiting for a signal, and trotted to the other side with his tail standing straight up. Gooder bounded over the road chasing after the cat and barreled into the shrubs. The girl rolled her eyes and then gestured for Mendel to go. The boy scuttled across, leapt elegantly over some bushes and disappeared. Sir Duffy was about to go when Felda signaled for him to wait. They both listened. Sir Duffy heard the clip clop and jingle of an approaching coach from the south and ducked back into the forest. Two panting horses pulled a coach at a walking pace. They were soapy with sweat and frothing at the mouth. Sir Duffy waited impatiently for the coach to pass, nervous at being separated from Mendel and the others.

As it came upon them, he peeked through the branches and felt a jolt of panic when he saw the Advanced Disciplines symbol embossed on the carriage door. To make things worse, the coach attendant pulled the horses to a halt right in front of them.

"Why have we stopped?" shouted a familiar voice from inside the carriage.

"The horses need to rest. We push them anymore and they'll drop dead," replied the coach attendant with authority. She opened a barrel of water crammed under her bench and filled an animal skin bag. The two weary beasts drank hard.

The door to the carriage opened, and Don Clapstone stepped out.

"I told you to change horses back at the city stables!" snapped the Don.

"You've dispatched all the horses to every part of the continent, Don! The only ones left in the stables didn't have the endurance to make this trip,"

The door to the carriage opened again and Don Woolstrum stepped out.

"That's fine, Latma. We could use a good stretch and some air." She yawned. "You are spreading everyone too thin, Horus. Yourself included. We can afford a break. You didn't even allow us time to change our clothes in Manuva."

He paced restlessly. "We must secure the heart. That oaf Duffy is the only thing standing between me and an advisorship in our Regula."

"We still aren't certain he has it. Or if any are even left on the continent. The majority of our agents feel this is all a wild goose chase, myself included."

"He has it all right. I can feel it in my bones. One sip of my tongue relaxer potion and he would have told me everything. But the law doesn't allow that yet."

She rolled her eyes. "Please spare me the details of your antiquated hobby. Old Regime alchemy should have died along with that wretched alchemist who started this whole thing."

Sir Duffy's eyes filled with hot tears. Felda reached over and put a gentle hand on his shoulder. The gesture kept him from throwing handfuls of nearby animal droppings at the two Dons, but it didn't ease his fear. Mendel was on the other side with two quarreling animals. The chill of fear circulated through his blood.

"And what if we do catch up with, Duffy? And there are no stones to be had?" asked Don Woolstrum.

"When we catch him we will indeed have the stones." He approached the coach attendant. "Once we reach our party, we won't need the horses anymore. They can rest all they want then." Latma threw the Don an angry look as he climbed back into the carriage.

"You can keep them at a walking pace for now," said Don Woolstrum as she climbed in after him. "Honestly, Horus. I think it's risky not to take horses the rest of the way."

"We won't be without the proper beasts."

They drove off, and Sir Duffy waited until Felda gave him

the signal that the carriage was out of sight. Then the two of them crossed the road, meeting up with the others.

"Oh me rattled wits," said Sir Duffy to Mendel, " you're all right over 'ere wif these two numbskulls."

"I saw the Advanced Disciplines people, Sir H. Where do you think they're headed?" asked Mendel.

"I'm not sure, but I don't want to wait 'round guessin'." Getting to the Great Lady was more important than ever to Sir Duffy. Being caught with the stone would lead to all sorts of criminal trouble for him. Avoiding Don Clapstone's experimental potion was crucial.

The traveling party pressed on, following Felda down a path. Butter deftly climbed a tree and leapt onto Gooder's back again. The horse tried to protest, but Sir Duffy gave him a sharp look just as he was about to nip the cat.

"Knock it off you two," snapped Sir Duffy.

They stopped at a small stream to wash up. Gooder pawed at the water, splashing himself and almost Butter. Then he moved to lie down in the riverbed, but Felda stopped him in time, saving the packs and the cat. Sir Duffy took off his coat, rolled up his sleeves and sank his arms and face into the cold, refreshing water. Clouds of dirt spread through the clear stream. The children washed up quietly, glancing at the path behind them often.

After everyone ate a quick snack, Felda led the party through the dense forest of iridescent trees and foliage. Clear leaves sprouted from white sparkling branches. Sir Duffy had always loved this particular forest. It looked as though it were made of many tiny crystals. However, he found it hard to appreciate at the moment. He felt as though he were being hunted, and tried not to imagine what would happen if he were caught.

They walked for a couple of hours before stopping in a fruit orchard to make lunch. Sir Duffy started the fire while Mendel picked red glittering apples and unpacked ingredients for a fruit medley stew. Felda disappeared into the woods briefly and returned with a dead comestible class pheasant that she de-feathered and butchered. She let Gooder and Butter eat the unwanted parts and then put the carcass on a stick over the fire. The boy added spices and oils to the stew.

Gooder kept nudging Sir Duffy until he took the packs off. The horse then disappeared into the woods to hunt his own meal. Butter weaved around Felda's legs and meowed until she fed him bits of crispy bird skin. Sir Duffy sat close to the pot, watching it bubble while he sorted his thoughts.

"Is it true Sir Duffy that you invented the reverserator antidote? The potion that can cure any poison?" asked Felda.

The alchemist shook away his troubles and looked up at the girl. Mendel sat next to her with his journal open to a blank page on his lap.

"Well, Sir Mostly was the one who figured out that coal miner's water draws out poison, but it isn't enough for catfink venom, so I kept experimentin' until I added the Smoky Raven eggs, which we knew stopped a number of poisons. I tested it out on a field rat that had ate some of that Advanced Disciplines rodent poison and the little stinker survived, but when I allowed the potion to sit for twenty minute, the next poisoned rat I found didn't make it." Sir Duffy tasted the stew and added another spice cube.

"Wow!" exclaimed Felda. "You've saved lives, Sir Duffy."

She leaned down and kissed the top of Butter's head. The cat cleaned its paws while curled up in her lap. "Someday I hope my work saves lives."

"Well, lives wouldn't need as much savin' if them Regula nuts weren't poisonin' each other." Sir Duffy snorted. "Wild catfinks rarely bite anyone. They are just these little cats that live up in the trees, mindin' their own business. They only bite when threatened, and these Regula profiteers pay good money for the venom, so dealers in the illegal trade 'unt the poor beasts." He frowned into the stew.

Felda hugged Butter to her chest. "I wish I could have saved my father's life."

Sir Duffy reached over and squeezed her hand. "I'm afraid not even my reverserator antidote could 'ave cured a necrodite infection. I mourned your father. Great man. Fought 'ard for us in the Regula courts. Got us some important victories. Like overturnin' the ban on candlethorn wheat. Nothin' treats joint pain better."

"How does someone get a necrodite infection?" asked Mendel.

Felda and Sir Duffy exchanged looks.

"No one knows how my father got it," said Felda. "Necrodite bacteria grows deep in the ground where there's no air. It can't survive anywhere else. Miners are the only ones who rarely ever get it. My father was nowhere near a mine." Anger filled her face. "Someone infected him on purpose." Butter began to lick her face.

They were all silent for a moment.

"Why are some people so rotten, Sir H.?" asked Mendel. "Like that woman, Don Woolstrum? I *thought* she was kind

141

of nice back at the shop, but what she said about Sir Mostly was cruel."

"Cruelty is a product of fear, my boy. They are afraid of Sir Mostly. I reckon they are afraid they can't do what he did."

The boy was stroking Esther, but she slithered down onto the ground. "What are you doing, Esther?"

"Not to worry. She's growin'." Sir Duffy chuckled. The gusselsnuff was the length of the boy's entire arm now and as thick as a chair leg. "They start to venture away once they get older and more comfortable. Let 'er explore. She won't go far."

Esther slithered only a few feet away and then sat in her S-shape, sniffing the air and looking around. The end of her tail felt around the ground, picking up pieces of debris and putting them down. Sir Duffy watched Mendel, who wasn't taking his eyes off the little creature, and chuckled. The gusselsnuff turned to the man and slithered over to him. She sat up again and let him scratch under her chin.

Gooder appeared from the trees. He snorted at the party, went to a tree and wiped his bloody snout on the sparkling bark.

Sir Duffy tasted the stew, stuck a fork in the pheasant and announced lunch was ready. They filled their bellies, sharing with their animal companions. After everyone finished, they cleaned up the camp and packed up Gooder. It was midafternoon. Felda informed them that they would reach the bird fields in about an hour.

Once they cleared the crystal forest, the deer paths became convoluted and split off in many directions, but Sir Duffy was confident in Felda's navigation. The new forest had a single species of giant grey trees. They had tall, thick trunks and long slender branches that curled in elegant loops like handwriting against the sky. Clusters of red leaves blotted out the sunlight.

Sir Duffy heard the bird fields well before they reached them. A cacophony of trills, chirps, caws and whistles built upon one another like a crescendo. Gooder's eyes widened and his nostrils flared. Butter paced in circles on the horse's rump.

Felda stopped the party several leaps from the tree line. Gooder reared with excitement. Sir Duffy grabbed the horse by the halter and patted his neck to steady him.

"So 'ow we gonna keep this bloody beast from tryin' to snatch birds?" asked Sir Duffy. "'E 'as never been fruw the fields before."

"We have to tie his muzzle and cover his eyes and lead him through," replied Felda.

"What 'appens if 'e snatches a bird?"

"It depends on the kind of bird. We could be dive-bombed by fat wobblers, swarmed by an entire flock of picky dancers, or ripped apart if he grabs a red chingsa."

"Will they attack if they see the 'orse?"

"No. As long as we move quickly and quietly without disturbing the flocks, they won't attack. The birds will let us pass because moving through the tall grass kicks up flying insects. So they will be diving close to us while catching bugs. As long as we keep our eyes down and limbs to ourselves they won't touch us."

While Felda tied and covered Gooder, Sir Duffy listened to the fields. At first it sounded like chaotic noise, but as his ears processed the sounds he could hear an orchestrated rhythm. There was a pulsating hum, a percussive caw, various songbirds singing notes in harmony. The high-pitched trill of the red chingsa punctuated the symphony. He couldn't help walking forward to see what was going on. Mendel followed him.

They moved near the edge of the field and stood in a gap in the trees, staring wide-eyed. The birds swarmed in clouds that changed shape and moved in synchronization. They saw billowing clouds of black, pulsating swarms of blue, darting yellowing streaks, and flowing in and around it all an unbroken stream of dancing red. The entire spectacle moved above a wide field of tall, uniform woodwind reeds.

The man and boy were so mesmerized by the sight that they didn't notice Felda and Gooder behind them. The noise of the fields was deafening. Sir Duffy jumped when he felt the horse's breath on the back of his neck. Felda had tied his muzzle shut with a leather band and wrapped dark cloth around his ears and eyes. Gooder threw his head up and around and pawed at the ground.

Felda signed "We need to hurry" with her hands. She tied a kerchief around her nose and mouth and handed Mendel and Sir Duffy kerchiefs to wrap around their own faces. They quickly did so, and followed her and Gooder. Felda's pack squirmed with agitation. Butter was not happy being trapped inside.

The tall, green reeds rose to just above Sir Duffy's head and gently clinked as he walked through them. He kept the boy in front of him and stayed close, worried the field would swallow him up. Gooder walked at an excited pace while Felda held him by the halter. Disturbed insects were jumping, flying and buzzing around their faces by the handful. Esther, poking out of the back of Mendel's shirt collar, snatched bugs out of the air and devoured them.

A bird flew right by Sir Duffy's head, startling him. Another swooped over the boy, causing Esther to retreat into his shirt. The alchemist noticed stray feathers tangled among the reeds and collected intact red chingsa plumage; they were a key reagent for a waterproofing potion.

More than a few times, wings grazed Sir Duffy's cheeks, but he continued to concentrate on trekking through the field. He glanced up and saw the layers of birds flying overhead. It felt as though the chirps, trills and warbles penetrated his whole body, vibrating up and down his spine. Suddenly he walked into Mendel, who had stopped because Gooder was rearing. Felda pulled the horse down by the muzzle and quickly mounted him, awkwardly sitting in front of the gear. Her pack looked possessed. Butter managed to get an arm out and swatted the air blindly. Sir Duffy cringed and waited for the birds to attack, but they didn't. Felda dug her heels into Gooder's side and got him moving forward with lurching, blind steps. A bird that moved too fast to identify snapped at Butter's paw, causing the cat to retreat. Sir Duffy urged the boy forward, and they continued through the fields.

The alchemist thought they were done for again when a red chingsa landed on Gooder's rump. It had a long orange beak, brilliant red feathers with a single purple feather on the tips of each wing. As it snatched at flying bugs, Gooder's tail searched for the intruder. The scaly appendage tried to grab the bird's leg, but Mendel snatched it in time and held on to it tightly.

The tree line came into view several leaps away. A fat green and gold bird landed on Sir Duffy's shoulder and swallowed a squirming bug held in its beak. He winced, hoping it wouldn't peck out an eye, but it was quickly gone. They reached the forest edge, but Felda kept them moving forward. Gooder fought Mendel's hand with the end of his tail and the boy finally released it.

They stopped within earshot of the fields, still listening to the music. Felda dismounted, released Gooder's muzzle and uncovered his face. The horse whinnied loud enough to be heard over the fields. Esther plucked an insect out of Mendel's hair and Sir Duffy plucked one out of his ear and laughed with relief. His mood improved after a little adventure and seeing such a spectacular sight. Just as he began feeling optimistic, a wave of uneasiness passed over him. At first he wasn't sure why, but when he saw the look of alarm on the faces of his companions he realized the field had gone completely quiet. He turned back toward it, but couldn't see much past the bracken of dark red leaves.

"Is that normal, Felda?" asked Sir Duffy.

"Not at all." The girl looked afraid.

Sir Duffy felt a prick of pain in his side and grabbed at it. Something sharp was vibrating in his pocket. He reached in and pulled out the shard of strange metal he had found in the tunnel. It was dancing and made a low-pitched hum. His blood went cold with fear.

"We need to get out of 'ere, now!"

They all moved with haste, following Felda down an over-grown path. His instincts signalled danger in great pulses of energy, and he knew better than to ignore them. He pushed the children into a run. When Mendel started to breathe heavily, he picked the boy up and set him atop Gooder's back. Felda trotted at a swift pace. The girl was hardier than Mendel.

Sir Duffy started to feel his age and weight, his belly cramped and his knees ached, but he forced himself past the fatigue. He had to get the children away from whatever was coming.

After they entered a new forest of lime green leaves and fat black trunks, the shard in Sir Duffy's hand went still. He put it back in his pocket. Felda led them down into a small valley where the canopy was thick and very little light shone. Sir Duffy made the party keep going a little longer at a quick walk before they came to a stop in a thicket of strong-smelling brandy bushes.

Mendel slid off Gooder's back, looking sore from the bumpy ride. He lifted his shirt to check on Esther, who was coiled around his midsection. Sir Duffy leaned against a tree, huffing and puffing, his face flushed and slick with sweat. He took a drink of water and looked over the boy.

"You all right, Mendel?" He squeezed the boy's shoulder.

"What happened, Sir H.?" Mendel sounded worried.

"A phenomenon. I can't explain what kind." He rubbed his temples, trying to wrap his mind around the occurrence.

"The fields only get quiet for a couple hours in the dead of night, but even then there are still owl hoots and night-eye caws," said Felda. She began to rub down Gooder, who had worked up a sweat.

"I fink someone or somefing silenced those flocks. 'Ow they did it and why is beyond me. But we won't light a fire tonight. Everyone stay close and stay quiet." Sir Duffy looked at Felda. "Do you fink you could do some backtrackin', make sure our tracks are covered?"

"I can. I'll hide and keep watch while you two get some rest. This is a good spot to camp for the night. We'll hit the

Thornfields tomorrow afternoon. Then we'll be safe." She finished cooling down Gooder and opened her pack. Butter was reluctant to leave it at first, but when the girl quietly disappeared into the forest he leapt out and trotted after her.

Sir Duffy only unpacked a few items from Gooder's back, in case they needed to make another run for it. He sat down next to Mendel. Esther was curled up in his arms, licking the salt from his face. They shared a bag of dried meat and fruit while Sir Duffy recorded the event in his journal. When he finished, he looked through Sir Mostly's journal to see if there was anything about the bird fields related to what he observed. He also wanted to know if Sir Mostly had ever encountered the strange metal found in the tunnel. There wasn't much light so he took out a small light globe to read by, slowly turning the old yet invaluable pages.

They camped under a large black tree. It was early evening. A low hum of insect violinists came from the surrounding forest. As Sir H. read Sir Mostly's journal, Mendel leaned against the tree and rotated the Diajob petals. He aligned the symbols for noise and silence, and stared at the configuration, trying to understand how all of those birds could suddenly go completely silent. He sketched the air with symbols, then crossed out and threw away the unbalanced equations. He tried several more attempts, but none offered any mathematical insight, leaving him frustrated. Then nature called to him, and he decided to answer back.

"I'll be just over here, Sir H. I have to go," he announced.

"Stay close," replied Sir Duffy, without looking up from Sir Mostly's journal.

The boy circumvented the black trunk of the obese tree. Its knotted, thick roots crawled and twisted in and out of the ground with the obvious intention of seeing Mendel fall on his face. On the other side he spotted a bush where he could do his business, and he did so with efficiency. Once he'd put himself back together, he suddenly froze at the thought that Felda might be watching nearby. He scanned the forest, but saw only trees and vegetation.

He began negotiating his way back around the tree when he heard the branches above shudder. He looked up. Felda deftly climbed down the knotted trunk.

"Everything all right, Mendel?" she asked quietly once she reached the forest floor. Butter leapt gracefully from a tree limb onto a branch stump and sat there, his belly hanging over the edge.

"How long have you been up there?" asked Mendel suspiciously.

"I didn't see anything."

Mendel considered her for a moment, deciding whether or not he believed her. Then he decided that it didn't matter because there was nothing he could do about it.

"Have you seen anything following us?" he asked. Esther popped her head out of his collar and purred a greeting to the girl.

Felda reached over and stroked the gusselsnuff and whispered, "No, but I saw a little bit of smoke in the distance, back towards the bird fields. Could be a hunter, but a hunter wouldn't silence the fields like that."

"What makes animals go quiet?" Mendel whispered back.

She thought for a moment, then answered, "Danger."

149

Mendel sketched a note with his pointer finger. Talking with Felda was helping him think. "What would be dangerous to a huge mass of birds?"

She thought longer this time and finally said, "Birds have many predators, but none of them are big enough . . ." She stopped and looked at Mendel with alarm.

"What is it?"

"The creature. The one from *the mistake*. The birds left the fields when the beast attacked. Even after Sir Mostly defeated it, the flocks didn't return for over a year."

Mendel lost his breath for a moment. His whisper grew louder with a trace of anger. "But the beast hasn't returned. Everyone would know if it did."

"I'm not saying it has. I'm only saying that's the only thing I can think of that comes close to explaining what happened." Her nostrils flared.

Mendel let his fear get lost in the chaos of his thoughts and focused on the logic of what she said. As far as they knew, there had only been one other time the fields had been silenced. She was right to include the information in their discussion. He jotted down the insight into his imagination.

"Good point."

She opened her mouth but then closed it. After a moment's consideration she said, "Should we say anything to Sir Duffy?"

"He already knows. He's been listening to us from the other side of the tree." Mendel had developed the habit of always knowing where Sir H. was, ever since his company became important to him.

They both heard Sir H.'s quiet chuckle. He slowly appeared, tip-toeing around the tangled roots of the tree.

"You two make good finkin' buddies."

"What do you suppose this means, Sir H.?" asked the boy.

"I'm not sure, son. But we need to keep our wits sharp and our people close. Stay quiet and only use small globes for light. We don't want to advertise that we're 'ere. Understood?"

The children nodded.

"I'll resume watch," Felda said. "I see very well at night, so rest easy, both of you." She patted Mendel on the back. The gesture relaxed him some. Then she quickly climbed the tree and disappeared into the foliage, Butter followed her, quietly meowing.

Mendel and Sir H. returned to camp and kept quiet. The alchemist managed to get Gooder to lay down and chew on a large bone instead of going off into the forest to hunt. The horse kept trying to pull the straps to the packs loose. Mendel loosened them for him. He returned his attention to his journal. Sir H. leaned closer to him.

"So what you learnin' from that Diajob so far?" he whispered.

Mendel whispered back, "Well, before when I told Esther to talk to the cappamorph, it made me think about relationships between species." The boy closed the book and pointed to the Diajob. "This is the symbol for animal life here, but the symbol for human life is in the same track so I can't put them directly in line with one another. But if I stop thinking about the clock as just direct relationships connected by straight lines, well then I can make endless connections." He traced the points of the star in the middle.

"I'm impressed. You're not letting conventions restrict how you fink 'bout fings. That's one of the most important qualities an alchemist can 'ave." Sir H. smiled. "Now why don't you

151

get some rest while Felda watches over us." The boy felt more comfortable knowing she was looking out for them.

"All right, Sir H. What about you? You should get some rest too."

"I will. I've got a few fings I need to put down in me journal first. Go on, don't wait up." Mendel curled up with Esther and quickly fell asleep.

He woke later to Sir H. gently shaking him. It was dark, but a sliver of light showed on the horizon. The boy rubbed his eyes hard. Esther wrapped herself tighter around his chest.

"Mendel, I need you to keep watch while I get another hour of sleep. You fink you can manage?"

He yawned and nodded his head, and Sir H. messed his hair.

"Good lad. It's been pretty quiet and Gooder is up lookin' for breakfast. Just pay attention to 'is behavior. If you notice any changes then wake us up."

The boy looked over at Felda, asleep under a bush with her feet sticking out. Butter appeared from under the same bush and commenced a series of stretches and self-bathing rituals.

"Go on Sir H. Get some sleep. I'm awake." Mendel yawned again while Sir H. laid his head down on his forager satchel.

The forest was mostly quiet except for some low, long whistles in the treetops. Gooder stood several steps away, rubbing the back of his ear on some branches. Sir H. began to softly snore.

Sitting down on a big fallen branch, Mendel chewed on a butter fig while he flipped his journal open to his note on the cappamorph:

The cappamorph's slime was sticky but it had no odor. Its skin looked clear but I could not see any of its organs. Other than the vibrations its skin made while changing, I didn't hear any commu-nicative noises. However, it seemed to react positively to Esther's purrs and coos. She must have used the common language Peatree spoke of. Though the literature has cappamorphs listed as fearful and skittish, this particular one seemed more motivated by curios-ity, which overpowered any fear it may have felt. This suggests they are part of the canny class of animals. I admit the interaction was exhilarating.

A snap of a twig made Mendel look up, but it was only Gooder searching through the foliage for critters. Esther unwound herself from Mendel's chest and came up for air. She yawned and rubbed her long upper body in Mendel's hair until she was completely awake. Then she slithered off him and onto the forest floor. This still made him nervous, but he was starting to get used to it, and had learned to watch her from the corner of his eye. She found a half-buried tuber, dug it out of the ground and sat in her S-shape, chewing on the root.

Mendel turned his attention back to his journal but saw with surprise that the pages were empty. He had forgotten that he had never written those notes down. He blinked a few times, and the writing reappeared in golden strokes. Mendel found the act of writing difficult, it took focus away from his thoughts. His imagination was easy and familiar to him. Every page had a number at the top that he attached to his imaginary notes. Since numbers were absolute, he could organize his thoughts easily by using them. He continued to think about Esther and the cappamorph:

Humans are not the only life forms that are interested in the world around them. Various non-aggressive animals and plants belonging to the canny class have shown interest in engaging with what they don't understand in order to gain knowledge of the world they exist in. That cappamorph wanted to know something it didn't previously know.

Mendel paused in his thoughts to summon a new one. He was excited to take animal behavior classes with Peatree. The idea made his stomach flutter.

Mendel dug into his forager satchel, pulled out a jar of pickled eggs and tossed one to Esther. He ate one of the sour eggs himself while trying to identify a small bird on a branch. Suddenly he felt as though Esther wanted something. He looked at the furry serpent. Her pickled egg lay in the dirt uneaten. Then he felt a very quiet vibration in his head. She wanted something sweet. Mendel reached into his bag and handed her a butter fig. Esther snatched it from his hand and chewed it.

The boy watched the gusselsnuff closely, waiting for the sensation to happen again, but it didn't. He wondered if that had been the low frequency language Peatree talked about. He didn't exactly hear the sounds. It was more like he felt them. He scribbled the occurrence down in his imagination.

Mendel packed away his journal. The chill of the morning gave way to sunlight that streamed through the bright green leaves in broken beams. Butter clawed at Felda's feet. The girl moaned and tried to gently kick the cat, but he kept pawing, and a half-sleeping Felda sat upright rubbing her eyes.

Gooder caught sight of the cat and froze, lowering his head in the hunting position. Butter stiffened and watched the horse with spite. Gooder lifted his front talon and the cat hissed and took off into the shrubbery, with Gooder in pursuit.

After they dragged Gooder back by the halter, they let Sir H. sleep a little longer while they packed up the few camp items.

"How long will it take us to get to the Thornfields from here?" whispered Mendel.

"We should get there by the afternoon. Once we do, whoever's following us won't be able to anymore."

"Why not?"

"The Kapathia crew were very clever. The opening is almost impossible to see unless you know where to look. It's an optical illusion."

"What if they see us entering?"

"They'd have to be right behind us, but I'll make sure they're not."

A curious thought occurred to Mendel. "Did you learn how to be a good land traveler from your father?'

A familiar look of anger crossed her face. "No." She was quiet for a moment. "My mother is the adept land traveler."

Mendel's brain calculated her emotions. "Your mother makes you angry."

Felda teared up. "My mother wanted to stay in the mountains, my father couldn't leave the academy. They split up. My mother insisted I stay with her for the summer, the summer my father died." She wiped her eyes. "It's her fault."

"What's her fault?" asked Mendel.

She didn't answer. Butter jumped into her arms and licked her salty tears.

Mendel started to feel something. It was an old emotion he hadn't felt in years, a sort of ache. *The thought* began to stir. He had an impulse to say something, and his brain told him that *the thought* would go away if he did.

"My mother makes me angry, too," he blurted.

Felda looked at him. "Why?"

The words came without his permission. "She couldn't love a Primore. She left before I could speak." *The thought* disappeared. "I don't know what it's like to have a mother."

Felda frowned. "I'm sorry that happened." She reached over and squeezed his hand.

"I'm sorry you lost your father." He squeezed back.

Mendel wasn't sure what to do next so he checked his thoughts for a task and went to wake Sir H. Felda finished securing their belongings to Gooder's back. Mendel knelt down next to the alchemist and gently shook him.

"It's time to get moving, Sir H."

At first the alchemist just mumbled and gave a few more snores, but after the second shake he opened one eye and sat straight up.

"It's all right, Sir H. It's just time to get going."

He looked at the boy and at his surroundings, and soon relaxed. Mendel smiled and helped his mentor up. Esther slithered up the boy's leg and draped herself over his shoulders.

The traveling party followed Felda along barely noticeable paths. Mendel quietly tried to get Esther to talk to him again by thinking at her. After no response, he tried to hum, thinking vibrations had something to do with it. The gusselsnuff ignored him. He thought more about their earlier exchange. It was peculiar how he had become aware of her emotions through his own feelings. This gave him an idea. He focused on feeling the need for her attention instead of projecting a thought at her. Esther's body perked upward and she looked at the boy. Delighted, he continued experimenting. He wanted her to move from one shoulder to the other. At first she used her tail to tug on his other ear. The next attempt had her sliding down his arm. When he finally focused on the feeling of her on his other shoulder she slithered over and perched herself there. His imagination quickly filled with notes. He bumped into Sir H. a couple of times while scribbling, making the alchemist laugh.

In the early afternoon, Felda told Sir H. that there was no sign of a follower, so he felt comfortable enough to let everyone rest briefly. They came to a clearing where several smaller black trees, uprooted by storms, had fallen over onto one another. Plenty of sunlight shone down onto short, lime-colored grass in the clearing, and they all sat and took in the warmth.

Sir H. drank from his water skin and caught his breath. Mendel noticed that his mentor had already lost a little weight from their trip. His round belly wasn't as round. Felda stripped off her grey leather coat, and spread it out on the grass and lay down. Her long silky hair flared out around her head and her light green eyes smiled at the sky, her mood improving. Butter curled up next to her and purred. The boy noticed how strong her arms were. Esther slithered through the grass, rolling around and rubbing her oily coat all over the soft reeds. Gooder nibbled at the citrus grass, which Mendel knew aided his digestion. He thought about getting out his journal but decided to just lay in the sun and watch the white clouds drift across the brilliant blue sky.

The forest was alive with twitters, chirps and songs. Just as the sun started to feel a little hot, a cool breeze blew over them. Mendel didn't realize he was falling asleep until Sir H.'s voice woke him up.

"We best be off."

Mendel frowned.

"I know. I could stay 'ere all day too, but we need to get to the Thornfields."

"We're almost there," Felda said. "The edge of the forest is just down this path. Then we'll cross the meadow to the thorns." She made a small gesture to Butter, and the cat jumped into her pack.

Mendel took one more look at the sky and smiled. Then he glanced at Sir H. and froze. The alchemist looked alarmed. It took Mendel a moment to realize that the forest had gone completely silent, Esther went rigid. Sir H. looked at the boy and then at Gooder and Felda. He grabbed Mendel and lifted him up, carrying him over to the horse.

"We need to run for it!"

Felda and Gooder snapped their heads around.

It was too late.

"Why in such a hurry, my dear alchemist?" The voice surprised them all. Sir H. froze next to Gooder and lowered the boy to the ground.

A woman stood on top of a fallen tree trunk at the edge of the clearing. She wore a heavy dark leather cloak with a hood, her pale hair spilling out over her chest and shoulders. Her skin was so white it was almost translucent, and her eyes were a color Mendel had never seen before, like a vanishing blue.

"There's no need to flee. We have so much to talk about." The stranger's voice was deep but still feminine, and had an unusual accent. Mendel clutched Sir H.'s hand, not sure what to do. The alchemist squeezed his hand and pulled him close.

The pale stranger raised a slender, dark metal staff, and a wall of gargoyle vines grew up between the two trees on either side of the path to the Thornfields. Mendel's stomach churned, and he heard Sir H.'s breath catch.

"What are you?" demanded Sir H.

"Just a stranger." She laughed. "And you are Sir Hennasee Ulfric Duffy. I have been looking forward to meeting you after all this time." Her eyes narrowed, and a wicked smile spread across her face. Her tone was malicious and playful.

"What do you want wif us? 'Ave you come to 'arm us?"

Mendel shifted to one side so that he could see the stranger better.

"Well that is entirely up to you, alchemist. You know what I want, and I know you have it."

"Even if I did 'ave it, what do you want wif it?"

"My kind has lived in the shadow of the beasts for too long. It's time they found the new home they have been looking for." The stranger held out her hand. "Hand it over now, and I'll spare you and the children."

"And if I don't?" Sir H. grabbed Mendel underneath his arm.

"I have one mission, alchemist, and I will stop at nothing to see it through. Your children notwithstanding." She stood unmoving, her eyes fixed upon Sir H.

Mendel realized that she was keeping to the shadows at the forest edge, and she had her hood up even though the day was fine. That made him think of a condition that occurred along the Cold Coast. During the long winter, the lack of sunlight turned some of the townspeople's skin very pale and gave them terrible headaches. Many would take trips to warmer parts of the continent, but they were temporally sensitive to the sun and needed to wear cloaks. This gave him an idea. Mendel turned to Esther.

"They're just kids," Sir H. pleaded. "Why don't you and me stay 'ere and talk 'bout this and we let the children continue on?"

"There is nothing to discuss, alchemist. You have a hard time following orders, I've been told." Her smile was full of malice. "Just like the time you killed that pegasus because you refused to do what your grandmother told you."

Sir H.'s mouth fell open.

Mendel concentrated on what he needed Esther to do. She looked from the boy to the stranger and then scanned the surrounding area. Very furtively, she slithered off his shoulders and into the grass, snaking quietly underneath Gooder and into the forest. Mendel noticed that Felda's pack had a missing bulge. Butter was nowhere to be seen.

"How could you possibly know that? What kind of creature are you?" Sir H. had tears in his eyes. He pulled Mendel closer to him and got a better grip under his arm.

"Soon you will know our damnation, alchemist. That is the only relevant information you need."

"You've got a lot more work to do, stranger. Damnation won't come easy 'ere. Too many good people in the way."

The stranger bared her teeth and raised her staff. The gargoyle vines crept out. One tendril twisted around Gooder's foreleg. The horse reared and the vine snapped off. Mendel felt himself being lifted by Sir H. and tossed onto the gear on Gooder's back. Faster than he could comprehend, Felda was sitting behind him, reaching over and grabbing the reins.

"Get 'im to the fields!" yelled Sir H.

The Quiet Way

Gooder reared again, but the gargoyle vines were tangled around the horse's legs and he couldn't get free. Sir H. tried to tear the vines away, but several thick tendrils got hold of his arm and pulled him to the ground.

"Sir H.!" yelled Mendel.

The boy tried to slide off Gooder's back, but Felda held onto him tightly. Then he heard the stranger scream. He looked up and saw Esther wrapped around her neck and Butter latched onto her leg. The stranger staggered into the light of the clearing, her hood had been pulled back. She screeched as the sunlight seared her skin. She dropped her staff, stumbled and fell to her hands and knees.

"Let go!" grunted Mendel. Felda's grip didn't give, but the vines did. Gooder reared and bucked, easily freeing himself from the gargoyle tendrils. Sir H. was standing too, pulling the limp vines off of himself.

"Get 'im outta 'ere!" cried Sir H. He pulled out the Putrid's Heart purse and threw it to Felda.

Suddenly a high-pitched squeal blared across the clearing. Though Mendel had never heard Esther make a sound louder than a coo, he knew it was her and that she was in terrible pain. The stranger had the gusselsnuff stretched out and writhing in her grip. Esther struggled to get free.

"No! Esther!" Mendel screamed.

The stranger threw Esther into the forest. Butter swatted her across the face, giving her a deep scratch. She tried to strike the cat, but he dashed after Esther. The stranger's pale skin was red, and her eyes were closed, streaming with blood. She found her staff with her searching hand, then crawled toward the shade.

161

"Felda!" commanded Sir H.

The wall of gargoyle vines had sunken low. Without any more hesitation, Felda reined Gooder toward the path. The horse leapt over the vines and galloped away, leaving Sir H., Esther and Butter behind.

"Felda! We have to go back!" pleaded Mendel.

She didn't reply. They burst through the edge of the forest in a great leap, landing in a meadow. Mendel almost fell off, but Felda steadied him. The Thornfields loomed dead ahead like a giant wall. At first it looked like Felda was going to run Gooder straight into the bladed branches, but she steered left and they galloped alongside the wall. Then she pulled hard on the reins, causing the horse to slide to an abrupt stop. Gooder reared, throwing his head in the air and whinnying. Felda jerked the reins, urging him to face the wall and walk forward. All Mendel could see was thick dark branches bristling with sharp blades that gleamed in the sunlight, and they were walking right into them. He imagined himself being sliced up like a block of cheese, and he put his arms up to cover his face. Gooder broke into a gallop, but Mendel didn't feel any cuts, so he opened his eyes. They dashed down a path that tunneled through the sharp branches.

"Felda! We have to go back and help Sir H.!"

The girl pulled the horse to a stop and quickly dismounted. With a few fast tugs on the straps, the gear fell off Gooder's back. Felda pulled Mendel down too, and the boy landed hard on his backside. She tossed him the purse.

"Stay here. Don't leave the thorns. I'll go back for them." Gooder started to leave without her, but she quickly jumped over his rump onto his back.

"No! Wait!" Mendel yelled, but Felda galloped off without listening.

Everything went quiet. The thorn forest creaked and loomed around him. The world suddenly seemed desolate, as though it had ended. Mendel waited in agony, pacing back and forth. He patted his arms and chest, feeling Esther's absence. *The thought* climbed forth from its dark place. He began to cry and swat at his leg. *You're all alone,* the thought said. *As you should be. You don't belong with those people. They are never coming back. They used this opportunity to free themselves from you.* Mendel sobbed and called out for Sir H.

"Please don't leave me! Come back!" He tried to find the entrance they had come in through, but the path split off in different directions. *Yes! Deep in the Thornfields, that's where you belong,* said the thought. Mendel ran back to the gear. He paced, crying and holding his hands over his ears.

The sound of snapping twigs made him jump. The noise came from deep inside the thorns. How could anything live inside such a deadly place? He heard clinking sounds, as though a metal can were skipping through the branches.

Mendel's eyes were flooded with tears, and his nose stuffed to the point where he could only breath through his mouth. His mind brimmed with the darkest thoughts. Was Esther dead? Had Sir Duffy left him forever? Mendel felt paralyzed. Would he be lost in the Thornfields, or would the stranger find him? *The thought* spoke. *Now you'll never get to be an alchemist.*

He wailed and covered his ears, his hands shaking. He took a deep breath and shook as he screamed with all of his power, "I *am* an alchemist!"

The thought went quiet. Mendel's emotions eased slightly,

and he looked around as though he might see *the thought* nearby. He was alone.

The ground rumbled. At first he froze. Was it the stranger using her staff to shake the continent? But then he saw Gooder galloping around the curve of the path toward him. Mendel cried and laughed simultaneously at the sight of Sir H. holding onto Felda's waist. The horse halted in front of him. He was soapy and wet with sweat, his mouth and nostrils flaring hard with each breath.

"Sir H.!" shouted Mendel. He ran to the horse's side and helped his mentor slide off. It was obvious he was injured. "I . . . thought . . . you left me," he sobbed, and wiped tears from his eyes. "Are . . . you hurt?" His nose was running, and his mouth quivered.

Sir H. hugged him tight with one arm. He was holding the stranger's staff in his other hand, and he leaned on it for support. "It's me ribs," wheezed the alchemist.

He released Mendel and reached inside his jacket. When he pulled his hand out, it was covered in blood, and he fell to his knees. The chaos of a million noisy, feverish thoughts inside Mendel's head froze in place, and gently cleared away. Clean equations appeared in golden strokes, and he knew what he needed to do to help. He opened his mentor's jacket and saw a long slash across his ribs. The blood stain on his shirt was growing. Sir H. opened the other side of his jacket and revealed a curled-up Esther cradled against his chest. Her eyes were half closed, and a long scratch stretched from beneath her chin to a quarter of the way down her underbelly.

Mendel dropped the purse in Sir H.'s lap, leapt to his feet and ran to the field kit, which had fallen on its side. Felda helped him push it upright and then stepped away to rub down Gooder to prevent the horse from overheating. Butter was on the horse's back, licking a small scratch on his rump. The boy opened drawers and extended shelves, plucking up bottles and vials and checking labels. He piled everything he needed into his shirt and dashed back to Sir H. The alchemist was wincing and wheezing while trying to keep pressure on the wound. Mendel sat down and rested the potions in his lap. He removed Sir H.'s hand and without hesitation ripped the slash in the shirt wide open. The gash was two-hands long but mostly shallow, except the initial point of entry which was one knuckle deep. The blood oozed slowly, which made Mendel less worried because that meant no major blood vessel had been cut. He poured water over the wound and blotted it dry with a sponge cloth. Esther whimpered from inside Sir H.'s jacket. The boy quickly opened a jar of brown searing powder and sprinkled it generously over the gash. The man gritted his teeth while the powder sizzled and turned into red foam.

Mendel let the powder work and turned his attention to Esther. He gently raised Sir H.'s jacket and found Esther licking the part of her wound she could reach. He slowly slid his hands under her shaking body and lifted her up. She whined and shivered. The boy cradled her in the crook of his arm and turned her over. She guarded the scratch with her arms, afraid of more pain, but Mendel stroked her face and body until she relaxed. Sir H. took from Mendel a vial of dark purple opius liquid, and pulled the cork out with his mouth and spat it out. He took a swig and grimaced, moaned, then sighed.

Esther's scratch wasn't deep either. He guessed it was

caused by the underbrush she was thrown into. Mendel plucked debris from her disheveled fur and unstopped a bottle of jewelup oil with his thumb. He coated his forefinger with the light-colored oil and gently stroked the gusselsnuff's wounded scales. She cooed, wrapped her tail around Mendel's wrist and licked the other fingers of his hand.

"We can't stop 'ere," groaned Sir H.

"We're all right here for the moment," said Felda. "I don't think she's following us. Gooder hit her pretty hard. And anyway, she won't be able to find the entrance." The girl was rubbing down the panting horse with concern.

Mendel coated a fingertip in the opius potion and let Esther lick it off. Once she finished, her shivering ceased. He examined the rest of her long body and found a few minor scratches that he treated with the jewelup oil. She held her body sort of crookedly so Mendel gently massaged her long torso. As he rubbed her lower ribs she jumped. They were badly bruised, probably when the stranger pulled on her. The boy deftly plucked a packet of yellow powder out of his supplies and blew a small pinchful into her face while focusing on wanting her to inhale it. She sniffed it in response and sneezed. Mendel tucked his friend inside his shirt and turned his attention back to his mentor.

Sir H. tried to sit up. Mendel pulled him forward and helped him get his jacket off. The red foam was mostly dried and crusty. The bleeding had stopped completely, but the flesh was still badly damaged. Mendel had Sir H. raise his arm over his head, which made him grit his teeth again. The boy used a sponge cloth to scrape off some of the dried foam. The man hissed. Next Mendel wet a clean sponge cloth with a bottle of fermented coda juice. As he patted the wound, Sir H. took deep breaths. Mendel finished his treatment of the wound with a coat of jewelup oil. Then he sprayed ginger pearl water from a small bottle with an atomizer up the alchemist's nose, making him cough and gag.

After some snorts, Sir H. said "That's much better. Good work, son." He grabbed Mendel by the back of the neck and gently pulled him close. "Don't ever, for one second, believe what that silly voice tells you. You belong wif me, and I will never leave you. I love you, boy." He touched his forehead to Mendel's and the boy flung his arms around Sir H.'s neck and hugged him tight. Tears were returning to his eyes when he heard his friend hiss again.

"Oh, sorry, Sir H." He released him.

"I'm all right." Sir H. held his arm close to his injured side. "We've got to go."

Felda had been walking Gooder back and forth along the path. The horse had settled some, but his coat was only half dry. "We have to keep Gooder at a walk while he finishes cooling down, otherwise his insides will get all twisted."

Mendel helped Sir H. to his feet.

"You done good, Mendel." Sir H. grabbed the boy's shoulders to steady himself. Mendel helped him stand straight and then picked up the stranger's staff.

"Here, Sir H. Use this." He handed the staff to his mentor. The material felt strange. It wasn't wood, but it wasn't like any metal he knew. It was tall and thin, with a long, striated cut near the top. The metal was dark in color with embedded red specs and elaborate designs etched down the entire length of it.

Sir Duffy took the staff and leaned on it. "We need to keep movin'."

Felda grabbed her pack and handed Mendel his own to carry. She only hauled Sir H.'s things onto Gooder's back. The riled cat paced up and down the horse's spine with his fur still sticking up from all of the excitement. The party limped down the trail in silence. Mendel kept checking on Esther, who fell in and out of sleep, twitching herself awake. Sir H. looked pale, his gaze a million miles away. The boy wanted to ask what happened back in the clearing, but he knew the alchemist was still trying to understand it himself. Sir H. looked deeply disturbed.

They often stopped for quick water breaks. Mendel tried to convince Sir H. to let Gooder carry him once his coat dried completely, but he just shook his head and moved the party along. The many paths of the Thornfields split and turned in different directions, but Felda confidently directed them through the deadly maze. There were no birds or animals in sight. The fields were eerily quiet. Once in a while Mendel heard the clinking noises deep in the groves, but he didn't think it was a good time to ask for a lesson on Thornfield animal life. He walked alongside his mentor, holding his hand and wishing for everyone to heal swiftly, including himself.

It was almost dark. The Thornfields looked black and wicked against the grey sky. In the distance they could see what was left of the daylight coming through the wide archway at the end of the path. Sir Duffy felt his side burn, itch and ache all at once. He fought against the pain, refusing more of the opius potion; he needed to stay alert. The pale stranger had shaken him to his core. Not only was her power over the surrounding plant and wildlife jarring and dangerous, but she knew private things about him. Sir Duffy ransacked his memory, trying to figure out how she knew about the pegasus.

It had happened when he was thirteen years old. Young Duffy had gone on a camping trip in the plains with his grandmother Esther and Sir Mostly. He had been feeling neglected because his grandmother spent a good deal of her time with Sir Mostly. It was supposed to be just him and his grandmother, but at the last minute she had invited Sir Mostly to come along. Young Duffy felt resentful.

They had been following a flock of pegasi for three days when they lost track of them. Something had disturbed their flight pattern. Sir Mostly found the tracks of a single pegasus and the party followed them. Esther's gasp startled young Duffy, who had been trailing behind the pair. His grandmother and Sir Mostly were looking down into a gully. Young Duffy heard a pained neigh and ran to his grandmother's side.

A dozen Advanced Disciplines officers in grey uniforms stood in a tight formation around a trapped pegasus. Pinned by a net, the horse thrashed and called out with a strange, loud whinny. She was white with blue wings, and had long fangs that went past her chin. Her front talons scraped the dirt and her back hooves kicked out in desperation. The officers seemed less concerned about the restrained pegasus and more concerned about the sky.

Shadows passing overhead distracted young Duffy. He looked up and saw the rest of the flock circling overhead. The officers who weren't tightening ropes and straps around the pegasus shot pellets from an odd device made from metal and wood. Every time a horse tried to land, the officers pulled the device's trigger and hit them with the hard pellets, sending the pegasi skyward. Young Duffy felt outraged. He tried to run into the gully, but Sir Mostly put an arm out and stopped him. This enraged the boy even more, but his grandmother spoke quietly.

"My boy, wait."

"I have an idea," said Sir Mostly.

Young Duffy resentfully squatted down with the others and listened to Sir Mostly's plan.

"Henny, stay here and wait for our signal, then draw the officers' attention toward you. Make as much of a scene as possible. Then Esther and I will sneak in from the trees on the other side and cut the lines to free the pegasus."

Young Duffy waited with little patience for the two alchemists to skirt the gully. All he could do was watch the female fight for her freedom. Her heavy breath kicked up clouds of dirt, her limbs shook with exhaustion, and her neck bled from rope burns. The sight brought tears to his eyes.

It was taking too long for his grandmother and Sir Mostly to go around the long way. Her cry made him cover his ears. He wanted to look away but he had to watch for Sir Mostly's signal. She was getting tired, and could only use her one front talon to fight. Loud shouts and whinnies showered down from the flock. One female swooped down low, but an officer shot her hindquarters. Young Duffy saw several wounds on the flying pegasus. Streams of blood ran down her legs.

He was shaking with anger and sadness. He still didn't see his grandmother or Sir Mostly on the other side. And then the trapped Pegasus collapsed and let out a defeated groan. His heart sank into his stomach. The boy Duffy couldn't wait;

he had to do something. He slid down the slope and into the gully. His momentum threw him right at the Advanced Disciplines officers and the pegasus. There was no time to think, only to react. He pulled a knife from his boot and ran for the horse. He reached the closest line in one leap, near her head. The officers and the flock were yelling, but he ignored it all. He desperately tried to cut the thick line, but didn't get even halfway through before a man and woman grabbed him by the arms. The boy steeled himself, but the two officers had tight grips around his wrists and shoulders. For an instant, he looked at the defeated pegasus. Her eyes were wide and wild with fear.

The two officers wrenched the boy off the line and dragged him away. Young Duffy saw his grandmother and Sir Mostly being held back by other officers. They were trying to reach him, though, and not the horse. Taking advantage of the distracted officers, the flock swooped down to attack. The officer in charge shouted orders, but no one heard her in all the chaos. She reached into her satchel and pulled out a black cylindrical object with a short fuse. The symbols for danger and caution were stamped on the side. Young Duffy was pushed to the ground by the two officers. She used a sparker to light the fuse, threw it in the air and yelled, "Down!"

All of her agents dropped to the ground and shielded their heads, and the two officers covered young Duffy with their bodies. There was a ground-shaking *boom* that vibrated the boy's skull. He heard screams from the flock, followed by a series of pops. A moment later, the officers let young Duffy up. A cloud of smoke hung in the air, and the flock was receding in the distance. The smoke cleared. Young Duffy pushed the officers out of the way, they were no longer fighting him. He ran to the pegasus and fell to his knees. She was dead.

The Thornfields darkened, the sun had disappeared. Remembering the incident made Sir Duffy's heart sink. His head hung low, and his feet dragged on the ground. The guilt and fear he now carried seemed to double. What troubled him most was that the stranger knew about the incident. At first he suspected the stranger was in collusion with the Academy of Advanced Disciplines and that she had heard the story from the officers. But the officers didn't know he had disobeyed his grandmother and Sir Mostly. They were the only people who knew those details. If the stranger got the information from them, it would have been many years ago. But then how could the stranger have been around for so long without anyone noticing? His mind couldn't parse the situation. His body hurt, and his head ached. Never before had he longed this much for his grandmother.

As they came closer to the opening at the edge of the Thornfields, Gooder's ears and head perked up. He stopped walking. The rest of the party stopped as well, wary. A tall woman with dark skin and broad shoulders stepped into the open with a bright light globe. Sir Duffy let out a sigh of relief, Gooder whickered and Butter meowed.

The horse trotted past Capri, and Butter leapt off his back and into the woman's open arms. Felda walked to within a few steps of her mother and quietly said hello without looking up. Capri frowned and tried to reach for Felda, but the girl walked past her, Butter jumped down and followed.

Sir Duffy shuffled slowly toward them, with Mendel at his side. Esther popped her head out from under the boy's shirt.

The Quiet Way

She seemed to be feeling better, though her eyes weren't fully open. A large party of almost two dozen people were with Capri. Women and men clothed in rough mountain wear stood around tents and campfires, watching with anticipation as the traveling party emerged. Capri immediately noticed Sir Duffy struggling and gestured for two people to help him. He stepped outside the fields and collapsed to his knees. The boy backed away as a large man and a broad-shouldered young woman with strawberry hair helped Sir Duffy to his feet. They carried him to a soft patch of grass and lay him down. Capri knelt by his side.

"What happened, Henny?" She held his hand. The light globe lit up her face. Her skin was smooth and dark, her big brown eyes surrounded with thick lashes, and her hair was black silk with a few streaks of silver, all pulled back in a long braid. The sight of her comforted Sir Duffy.

"The pale—" His voice caught in his throat. Capri gestured, and a young man brought a skin of water. She held Sir Duffy's head up and tipped water into his mouth. He drank a few gulps and nodded when he'd had enough.

"You encountered the stranger?" asked Capri.

"Yes. She has some kind of power over plants and animals. And she wants the stone. She means to call the beasts." Sir Duffy wiped his forehead.

"Did she get the stone from you?" Capri had panic in her voice.

"No." Sir Duffy patted his jacket pocket.

Capri relaxed her jaw. "Good work, Henny. Your grandmother would be so proud of you." She kissed his forehead.

Sir Duffy began to cough, and he winced at the pain in

his side. Capri opened his jacket and looked at the wound. Concern crossed her face, and she felt his forehead.

"You need rest and nourishment." She turned to the woman at her side. "Get a stretcher and carry him to the middle tent."

It was too dark for him to see the mountains close by, but he could feel them looming over him. A steep mountain path still stood between him and the Great Lady. The stone felt heavy against his chest.

"We've got to get the stone to the Great Lady. Now." Sir Duffy struggled against his exhaustion, but Capri put a soft hand on his cheek.

"Calm yourself. We'll get to her tomorrow night. I have twenty women and men with me. You and yours will be safe. We'll get you and the stone to her soon enough." She stroked his cheek. Sir Duffy pointed to the stranger's staff.

"What is it?" she asked.

"'Er staff. That's the stranger's staff. It has somefin' to do wif 'er power."

Capri picked up the long staff. She looked it over. "We'll see if the Great Lady recognizes this metal." Capri handed the staff to a large woman with curly black hair, and quietly gave instructions. Then she turned back to Sir Duffy and smiled. He smiled weakly and squeezed her hand.

"I am so grateful for you and yours, Capri."

"And I don't know what we'd do without you." She kissed his forehead again, which was damp with perspiration. Sir Duffy felt safe enough to give in to his exhaustion and fell asleep.

He woke in the middle of the night. At first he panicked at the sight of an unfamiliar canvas tent and the sound of witch owl hoots, but the outline of Mendel and Esther asleep next to him in the dark snapped his wits together. He reached into his jacket pocket and felt the purse with the stone and relaxed. Then he took out a small light globe and shook it. The boy and gusselsnuff were sound asleep.

He lay awake, his mind unsettled. The trials of the journey north troubled him a great deal. Doubts of his strength to safeguard secrets and dangerous artifacts crept into his consciousness, but those doubts called forth a vivid memory.

Young Duffy was nineteen. It had been two years since the defeat of the great winged beast and the death of Sir Mostly. The new government was implementing more laws and regulations every week, and throughout the continent, citizens were repairing their damaged towns and cities. Sir Esther Duffy's heart was failing. Young Duffy traveled with her back to the Northern Forests.

Their people greeted them with great affection and care. They had preserved her home with the anticipation of her return, not a book or bottle out of place. The great magnalith trees of the Northern Forests were the largest on the continent, towering over the people like magnificent cities. Most tree trunks were as wide as houses, if not wider. The upper parts of the trees' roots grew above ground in beautifully twisted braids and knots. The foresters built their homes inside the root mounds, always being sure to give great care to the trees that sheltered them.

Esther Duffy's home stood atop a hill that overlooked the busy center of their village. Two very old, thick roots split from their braid to form an archway that framed a stained-glass door. Young Duffy stepped through and entered a large alchemy room full of tables and shelves littered with bottles, jars and cauldrons. A small fire was set in the fireplace, and a kettle whistled over it. He removed the hot water and found tea settings on a table. After making tea he checked on his grandmother. She was asleep on her bed beside a large window that overlooked the village below. A great beam of sunlight that had broken through the canopy shone upon her.

Her long grey hair was scattered across her pillow and shoulders. Young Duffy took a seat beside her. She breathed in shallow breaths. His grandmother had lost a good deal of weight. Her eyes were dark and sunken. He moved a strand of hair from her face, and her gentle blue eyes opened.

She smiled. "Ah, good. I'm still alive."

Tears filled young Duffy's eyes. "Of course you're still alive."

"I 'ave somefing to give you my dear boy. Once you get the tea that you forgot in the kitchen, you boob."

Young Duffy snorted and got up to fetch the tea. He grabbed a bottle of her heartwarming elixir and returned to her side, pouring the tea and adding the potion.

"We came 'ere to fix you up and restore your 'ealth, and that's what we're goin' to do," he said.

"I'm afraid the condition of me 'eart is beyond our knowledge. Charles devoted a good deal of 'is work tryin' to cure it, but I'm sorry to say me 'eart's done fightin'."

Young Duffy held her hand and covered his face with it, sobbing.

"Oh my dear boy, do not grieve for me too long. There is so much for you to experience in this life. I would 'ate for you to miss one second of it." She pulled his face close and kissed his cheek. "Now. I must give you somefing of great importance, lad." She pointed to a small set of drawers by the end of her bed. "In the top drawer you will find a wooden box. Bring it to me."

He gave a great sniff and retrieved the box. "What's in 'ere, grandma?"

"Secrets, my dear Henny. And they are quite the burden so I don't 'and 'em over wif pleasure but rather wif trust." She took the box in her lap and gestured for him to help her sit up.

"I promise I won't let you down, grandma."

She laughed. "You don't even know what promises I'm goin' to ask of you yet. But 'ere you are, ready and willin'. And that's why I love you so dearly." She squeezed his hand, then slid back the lid of the box. She took out something flat wrapped in a red velvet napkin. It was a journal.

"The first secret I am givin' to you is this." She handed it to him. "As far as anyone is concerned, this journal went wif Charles. The information in these pages are what saved us all. But this information, in the 'ands of someone wif the wrong intentions, can *kill* us all."

Young Duffy slowly turned the pages. More tears ran down his cheeks. After two years he still grieved for his beloved mentor. "I will treasure it." He sniffed.

His grandmother took from the box a large coin purse, untying the string. "These are the next secret I'm afraid I must burden you wif, love." She tipped the purse into the young man's hands.

He was stunned. "I can't keep these safe, grandma! There 'as to be someone else you can trust."

"Nonsense. You are quite capable. I know this for sure. And it's not just that I trust you, Henny. It's that I 'ave the utmost confidence in you. One day you will fully realize and understand your potential, and then you will understand why I chose you for this." She put the stones back in the bag. "Now. You must keep these out of the light. Study the notes, memorize 'em so you don't need 'em in order to act. And always keep 'em 'idden but close by, unless someone, any-one, starts lookin' for 'em. If or when that 'appens, take one of the stones and 'ide 'em in a cave in the Truegone Valley. You'll find Charles' notes on the cave in the journal. As for the second stone." She reached into the box and unwrapped a silver object.

"What is that, grandma?"

"This is a gift. Somefin' to remember me by. It's the symbol of our community. People you can trust. Remember that you can always rely on our people. When the time comes, bring the second stone to the Great Lady. Our people will 'elp you get the stone to 'er. But do not seek 'er out unless the stones are in danger. She is in 'idin'."

"I don't know if I can do this wifout you, grandma. Please don't go." Young Duffy lay his head in his grandmother's lap and sobbed. She gently stroked his curly brown hair.

"There is nofin' to be done about me departure, me love. I won't be gone for good. You will 'ave me voice in your 'eart." She bent down and kissed the top of his head. "Promise me, my dear boy. Promise you will carry this secret, guard it against enemies, and choose your loved ones wisely, for you need to trust every one of 'em as I trust you."

He tried to stop crying and took a few deep breaths. Finally he was able to say, "I promise, grandma."

He fixed dinner and they stayed up late talking of the great days before *the mistake* and the many adventures they had together. The next morning Esther Duffy died in her sleep.

Sir Duffy's mind came back to the dark tent. Tears quietly rolled down his temples. He gave a great sniff and tried to sit up, but a sharp pain reminded him of his injury. He peeled back his jacket and saw that someone had cleaned and re-dressed the wound. It was warm to the touch and very itchy, but Sir Duffy knew not to scratch it. He was surprised to feel the coolness of his forehead. Capri must have given him something for the fever.

He rolled onto his good side, untied the tent flap and pulled it open. It was very dark outside, but a small pile of embers smoldered several paces away. Sir Duffy had to squint to make out the two shapes sitting next to the dimming fire. He saw the strong, tall figure of Capri and the thin frame of a man.

He and Capri had always been good friends during their academy years. She studied weather, animal migrations, and hunting at the School of Nature. They spent summers together in the plains. Eventually she spent less time in Manuva and more time in the mountains. He didn't see her as often. Their friendship and affection always remained strong, though.

Two more figures appeared next to the fire to relieve Capri and the man from sentry duty. She left the fire and walked towards the tent. He shook his light globe.

"Causing trouble?" whispered Sir Duffy. They both smiled.

"I want to check your dressings again before I get some sleep."

Capri entered the tent, knelt beside Sir Duffy and pulled back his jacket.

"What did you give me? My fever is gone."

"I've kept up my alchemy studies all these years. You and Baz were good teachers." Capri took a bottle of brown liquid from her satchel and handed it to Sir Duffy.

He uncorked it and sniffed. "Blackened deer bile. It's fatal if not prepared properly." He took a tentative sip and smiled. "You are skilled at whatever craft you turn your attention to, my friend." He took a few more sips and replaced the cork.

"It helps to be good at many skills rather than be exceptional at a single occupation." She peeled the dressing and examined the wound in the dim light. "It's healing well. It must itch like mad."

"I've imagined settin' it on fire a couple times." They both laughed.

"I have some arctic cubes."

"You are merciful."

She extracted a couple of the chilly cubes from her satchel, crushed them in her hand and mixed in several drops of slug oil. Sir Duffy sighed deeply as she applied the mixture over his wound.

"There now." She prepared fresh dressings. Her friendly expression changed to a more worried one as she worked. "Henny?" He didn't look at her or respond, but silently nodded. He knew what she was going to ask. "Felda told us what happened. She said how she found you. The stranger had you by the throat up against a tree. How could someone half your size be so strong?"

Sir Duffy looked over at the sleeping boy next to him and listened carefully. Mendel's breathing was slow and steady.

"I don't know." He frowned. "'Er power . . . that staff . . .

I can't comprehend it, which makes me afraid." He clutched his chest. "She screeched at the touch of sunlight. Felda and Mendel were out of the clearin' by the time she crawled back into the shade. 'Er skin 'ad burns. I grabbed Esther. The poor fing was tangled in the shrubs, trying to get free, howlin' for Mendel. I tore at the vines in a panic, Butter jumped in and 'elped to free 'er. I made a run for it wifout lookin' back, I was so afraid, Capri." She squeezed his hand. "But then vines sprung up 'round me feet and wrapped 'round me ankles. I've never seen gargoyle vines behave so aggressively.

"I fell to the ground wif Esther in me jacket. Took all me balance not to land on 'er. I rolled onto me back and the stranger was there, standin' over us wif that awful staff. It was singin' somefin' 'igh pitched and those red specks were glitterin'. We was in the shade but only a few feet from the sunlight. I was 'bout to roll into the light, but the vines grabbed up 'round me arms and pinned me down. I thought that was it. I was done for. But Esther," he reached over and stroked the sleeping gusselsnuff. She purred and nuzzled Mendel's neck. "She slithered right quick up the stranger's arm and bit 'er 'ard on the 'and. She yelled somefin' fierce and dropped the staff. I felt the vines go limp and tore me way out of 'em.

"I went for the staff, but the stranger got there first and used the wicked fing to slash me ribs. Then she used it to push me up against a tree. It was like gettin' 'it by a carriage. I couldn't move against it. Then she grabbed me neck. That felt more like a normal person's grip. I don't know what to make of it all." He paused for a moment. "Me vision was goin' dark. I remember the look in 'er pale eyes. She was furious, but also amused. I thought all was lost, when Felda came ridin' in with me hero Gooder." A look of concern crossed his face. "Gooder! I forgot—"

"Your horse is fine. Better than fine, actually. He was quite excited. Poor Butter. Gooder chased him around, nipping at his tail. Took him a while to settle down. But once he saw the bone meal . . ."

Sir Duffy chuckled. "I do love that 'orse. But don't tell 'im that." His smile quickly faded. "That 'orse saved me life. 'E slashed 'er 'ard across the back. She dropped the staff and I felt like a carriage rolled off me. I found Esther wrapped 'round the staff. I scooped up bofe of 'em, and Felda swung us up on Gooder's back, Butter jumped in 'er lap, and we tore outta there like the beast itself was on our tail."

Sir Duffy's eyes felt heavy. The spring air was warm and the night insects were humming a soothing tune.

"You're a brave man, Henny. Esther Duffy was right to trust you with the stones."

Sir Duffy scoffed. "If it weren't for the kids and the animals I would 'ave never of 'eld onto 'em."

She squeezed his shoulder. "Exactly, Henny. She chose you because of the way people love you. And the way you love them back. Those bonds are what protect us."

Sir Duffy's eyes began to water and he looked over at the sleeping boy. "Nofin' can 'appen to 'im, Capri. I should send 'im 'ome to Abylant."

"Your love will protect him, Henny." She stroked Mendel's hair. "You need a boy of such significance. Just like I need Felda to help get me through it all."

"You've done right by 'er. That kid 'as your fearlessness."

Capri frowned. "According to her, she's nothing like me." She lowered her eyes. "This is the first time I've seen her in a year, and I barely got a hello from her."

"I'm sorry you lost Baz. She's mourning 'im, that's all. I felt mad at everyone when me grandma died."

"Part of me feels like I deserve it. I knew Baz was caught up in something serious with the Regula. That's why I wanted her here, in the mountains. I didn't want anything to happen to her. It was selfish of me."

"Don't blame yourself, Capri." He grabbed her arm and squeezed. "The only person who did anyfin' wrong is the one who gave 'im that infection. You, Baz and Felda are all their victims. It's never a victim's fault."

Capri tried to smile. "It's hard being separated from her like this. Not just by distance. You know what I mean?"

Sir Duffy nodded. "Let 'er mourn. She'll close the gap when she's ready. She's a smart kid. And capable. Just like 'er mother."

Capri laughed quietly. "She exceeds my capabilities. There is something very special about this generation of kids. Have you noticed?"

"Not until the boy came along. But once I saw it in 'im, I began to see it more and more. Especially at the academy. That's why I fink it's important I go back and start teachin'. What do you fink it is?"

"I don't know. The news of this stranger and what the Advanced Disciplines have been up to make me think that something wicked is coming. But these children and their stronger connection to our world fills me with hope."

Sir Duffy squeezed her hand. "There's 'ope in these kids.

You're right. I need the boy. I can't survive wifout 'im." Sir Duffy looked over at Mendel. "Once we get this stone to the Great Lady, I fink we'll all feel a little more easy. Me grandma told me stories 'bout 'er. 'Ow intelligent she is and everyfin' she did for us durin' and after *the mistake*. It will be somefin', gettin' to meet 'er after all these years."

"She will not disappoint you. Get some sleep. We'll ascend the mountain in the morning." She finished his dressings and was about to leave when a thought struck. "I almost forgot. A letter from Johan arrived by quick post this morning." She reached into her worn leather jacket and pulled out an envelope. Sir Duffy took it and said goodnight.

He opened the letter with sore hands, hoping it was good news. It was not. Johan's handwriting was rushed and messy. Sir Duffy had to read the note three times in order to understand it.

> Henny,
>
> After much inquiry and investigation, appears someone using old tunnels below school. What's more, books and a map have gone missing from library. I dearly hope this letter finds you and yours well. And I am most sorry if my lack of vigilance has cost you anything. Forgive me.
>
> Also, Sir Lovington wanted me to deliver a message to the boy. She said that the symbols he showed her are Primorish and have something to do with inheritance. Doesn't have anything more for now.
>
> With great affection,
> Johan

184

Sir Duffy folded the letter and placed it in his pocket. The news disturbed him. Had the stranger been lurking around the campus while they were there? How long has she been using those tunnels, and what kind of information had she acquired? These thoughts looped in his mind as he drifted to sleep. The alchemist shifted anxiously as he slept, and he woke up often in a sweat. The stranger haunted his dreams.

The Great Lady

Mendel woke to the sounds of footsteps outside the tent. He wiped the sleep from his eyes and tried to remember where he was. When it all came back to him, he felt for Esther and found her curled under his arm. He stroked her silky fur. She slid up and around his neck and nibbled his ear. The boy gently lifted her and examined the wound on her belly. It was healing well, some new scales were growing over the damaged ones, but he thought that it would probably leave a scar. He kissed the top of her head and sat up.

Sir H. had risen already, and Mendel heard his voice outside. He grabbed his satchel and crawled out of the tent. The sight of the mountains in the light took him aback. Blackened, ashy rock outcrops rose high above him. He couldn't see the peak, it was too far away. The mountain seemed as infinite as the sky. The base camp occupied a small scrap of grassland between the mountain and the Thornfields. The confinement made Mendel feel anxious. He worried that the stranger might find her way through the thorns and trap them against the edifice. But then he caught sight of a few horses lined up near a path that disappeared into the rocky crags. The option of escaping on horseback up the mountain eased his tension.

The sun was below the Thornfield horizon so Mendel knew it was still early. Women and men walked with purpose throughout the camp, putting out fires, packing away gear, and saddling horses. All of the tents had been packed up except for his. Two people collapsed it behind him and worked on packing it away. He wandered through the camp trying not to crash into people and horses. Esther perched in an S-shape on his shoulder, her skinny arms folded across her sensitive underbelly. Mendel found Sir H. sitting by a dead campfire eating stew. He waved the boy over.

"'Ere. I saved you a bowl." The alchemist handed it to him.

"Thanks, Sir H." He took a seat. "When do we start the climb?" Mendel alternated between spoon-feeding himself and Esther.

"Quite soon. Capri has insisted we share an 'orse. Usually I would argue, but given our reduced state, I've agreed. We want to make good time, and me 'obblin' along will slow the party down. And there are parts of the path that get narrow and deadly, so I'll feel better if you're on 'orseback wif me."

Mendel nodded. "Where will we find the Great Lady?"

Sir H. smiled. "At the top. We've got a lot of climbin' to do."

Mendel swallowed the last spoonful of stew and let Esther lick the bowl clean. Then Capri's people packed up the last of the gear, and Mendel was lifted up onto the back of a large chestnut horse with a long white horn. Sir H. sat behind him. Gooder stood in front of them with all of their gear tied to his back. The caravan of horses were a muddle of different colors and sizes. A large dapple grey towered over a strawberry roan pony that playfully nipped at his hocks.

Many of Capri's people rode, but some were on foot, Felda being one of them. She followed toward the back. Capri shouted a command from the head of the line, and the party moved. Mendel leaned forward as they approached the first bend of the path, curious about the inside of the mountains. Their horse turned the corner and walked into pitch darkness. They had entered a narrow cave. Mendel felt Sir H. grip his arm. They soon came out the other side, and Mendel had to clutch the horse's knappy mane when the path rose steeply in front of them.

It felt like the horse was almost vertical for a while. Mendel clung to him with his arms and legs. After an hour, his limbs were beginning to shake, and when he thought he might lose his grip, the path leveled out as they reached a plateau. Mendel had been so focused on staying on, he hadn't noticed how high they had gone. He peered over the uncomfortably close edge and saw nothing but a deep, dark crevice. Grey ash dusted the burnt rock around him. Tall, dark spires surrounded them and stretched upwards into patches of sky. White tree skeletons stuck out of charred rock shelves, and piles of dusty bones filled old fissures.

"Sir H.?" said Mendel. "Did the creature do all of this?"

"I'm afraid so. The retavic deer 'ave made quite the comeback, though. Look over there." He pointed to the steep slope nearby.

Mendel didn't see anything at first, but then he caught sight of movement on the slope. A large herd of deer balanced precariously all along the ridge. They had thick, dark coats and black antlers. Their hooves looked as though they were balancing on nothing. The herd grazed on black moss growing up the side of the mountain.

"That corpse moss feeds on the ash. It's been growing like mad all these years. The deer adapted to climbing the mountains long ago, but they fed on a different moss that doesn't exist anymore. That corpse moss came in a couple years after *the mistake* ended. The deer would have starved if it hadn't. Now they are flourishing."

Mendel scribbled notes into his imagination and watched the deer. They had passed rather close to a few, but the deer merely looked up at the passing people and, determining they had no business with them, resumed eating.

After another steep climb, Mendel saw that the path ahead was even for a good while, so he retrieved his journal. Esther slithered around the horse's back, combing through his fur and eating whatever she found.

Mendel opened the empty pages. He blinked a few times, and the golden letters appeared on the paper. He reviewed his notes about the stranger's sensitivity to light and speculated about the cause of her condition. The illnesses he knew of that caused such a reaction were temporary in nature and less severe, and there was something about the stranger that told him her condition was permanent. The boy wasn't able to surmise much more. His notes then moved to her power over the different plants and animals through the staff. He was more curious than alarmed. He thought about the gargoyle vines in the hallway back at the campus and how they politely wrapped themselves around his thumb. They also shook the globes. The canny class plants wanted to do things for people, he thought. He remembered what Peatree said about how no one truly had power over animals. That it is about communication and respect, and also awareness of their needs and fears. Why would the stranger be any different?

Mendel stroked Esther's chin. She let go of a fistful of horse hair and slithered up his shoulder to the top of his head. The boy smiled at the tickling sensation as she groomed her way through his hair. Turning his attention back to his journal, he underlined the word "power" with his forefinger.

Then he closed the journal and admired the Diajob on the front cover. Something about the sight calmed him.

"Oi!," Sir H. suddenly spoke. "We're about to climb again. Grab some 'orse 'air."

Mendel clung to the horse once again as they shifted to an almost vertical angle. They clamored up several more inclines, each one steeper than the last, only getting short breaks over more even ground.

Close to sunset, the suffocating rock faces gave way to a larger plateau under a brilliant sky. The mountain range stretched out before them, black summits against dark blue sky. Recovering emerald green valleys could be seen tucked away in deep corners. In the center of the range stood the collapsed Blackburn Volcano. Its base was wider than all the other mountains, and what used to be the highest peak was now a sunken crater covered in a thick layer of ash. Mendel took in the view from atop their horse with his mouth agape. A bug flew into it and he coughed.

Capri called for a short break. There was enough space for the caravan to spread out a little. Their horse wandered willfully to one of his companions, a yellow stud with a black mane. Gooder followed and helped Sir H. dismount by pulling on his pant leg with his mouth.

"You blasted 'orse! You're pullin' me pants off!" hollered the alchemist.

Sir H. winced when his feet touch the ground. Mendel slid onto the soft grass and helped his friend hobble away from the socializing animals. His own limbs felt sore from continuously clutching the horse. Sir H. and Mendel found an unoccupied patch of grass and milled there together with Gooder. The horse kept nudging the alchemist affectionately. The man reached back and patted him reassuringly on the muzzle.

Esther slithered into the grass next to Mendel's feet and plucked a few reeds. Then she retreated back onto the boy's shoulders and nibbled on the green shoots. She shivered slightly, and Mendel stroked her. He closed his eyes and let Esther know that she was safe. Soon he felt the uncanny vibration inside his mind and heard the gusselsnuff say her whole body hurt. Mendel's eyes flew open. He dug into Sir H.'s pockets and retrieved the vial of opius potion. Esther licked the purple liquid from his finger and quickly ceased shaking. He stroked her chin, and she began to purr. She told him 'thank you' in her native tongue and nibbled his ear.

The sky behind the mountains turned red as the sun sank behind them. The air had a slight chill to it, but the rock wall that the plateau stood against gave off heat. Mendel leaned on it and warmed himself. Sir H. kept away, though. He was sweating a little. The boy watched him sip blackened deer bile from a bottle.

Mendel was watching the sky change colors when he suddenly noticed that the horses were restless. At first he thought they just wanted to keep moving toward home, but then he saw the chestnut horse try to herd his companion toward the path with sharp bites. A woman pulled them apart. He looked around the camp, feeling uneasy. Butter stood on Felda's shoulders with his hair standing up. Capri looked over the caravan with concern. Then Esther darted into his shirt. He thought he heard her say 'hide.'

He ran to Sir H.'s side and pulled on his sleeve.

"What is it, son?" asked Sir H.

"Something's wrong. We have to get out of here," said Mendel.

Sir H. looked around, and the same look of concern crossed his face. Gooder nudged the alchemist in the back and pushed him in the direction of the path. His nostrils flaring.

"Mount up! Now!" yelled Capri.

Everyone scattered for their horses and packs. Loud bellows and wet growls came from below the cliff. The people froze. Mendel watched the edge of the plateau.

A massive, leathery hand with sharp talons grasped the lip of the cliff. A long trunk appeared next to it, and then the other hand. A gigantic creature pulled itself up onto the plateau, its short ivory tusks scraping the rocks. It trumpeted a loud call that echoed off the mountain side. It was a hellephant, and on its back rode Don Clapstone and two other Advanced Disciplines agents.

Capri yelled for the caravan to get to the path, but it was too late. Another hellephant climbed up on the other side of the plateau and blocked the way. Two more appeared behind them, all carrying agents. More creatures climbed up over the cliff edge and onto the level ground—mountain wolves

in leather harnesses. A few agents jumped down from the hellephants and grabbed hold of the wolves' leashes. All of the caravan horses snarled and whinnied at the beasts, and quickly formed a line between their companions and the intruders. Gooder stood directly in front of Sir H. and Mendel. The alchemist leaned on the boy. He was shaking.

The agents and their creatures faced the line with ready aggression. Capri jumped onto the back of the largest horse and stood up high in the stirrups.

"State your purpose here!" she yelled.

"We've come to search your caravan," said Don Clapstone. He held onto the large ear of the biggest hellephant and climbed to the ground. "We have good reason to believe you are harboring an illegal item. Our Regula has authorized us to retrieve the item and arrest whomever possesses it or interferes with its retrieval."

Capri steadied her horse. "Your institute does not have that kind of authority. And not even you could change the laws that quickly."

"You are ignorant of my authority!" Don Clapstone sneered at her. "When it comes to protecting our world from the likes of you I have every authority."

She stared Don Clapstone down. "We have every right to defend ourselves against unlawful attacks. Let us pass or suffer the consequences."

"You are outmatched, fool. I know you are transporting Duffy, and I know he has the Putrid's Heart. Hand him over, or you will all pay for your transgressions."

Mendel's blood went cold. There was nowhere for them to go.

"You have no evidence and therefore no right to search us. We *will* resist you," countered Capri.

Don Clapstone hissed through his teeth. "Fine then. Let the reckoning begin." He waved his arm, and the hellephants stepped forward.

Ready for a fight, the horses instantly leapt toward them. One of the agents yelled, "Fire!" Long metalwood bows snapped and unraveled compact balls of rope. Before any of the horses could strike a target, nets rained down on them. Bolos made of rope and metal flung through the air and wrapped around their legs. Capri's horse tried to rear, but his legs caught in a net and he fell forward. She barely jumped away in time before the horse fell on top of her. After tumbling a couple of paces away, she got to her feet and ran to Sir H. and Mendel.

"We have to get you two out of here," she said.

"There's no where to go," wheezed Sir H. He was having trouble breathing.

Capri's people tried to free their horses, but the agents let the wolves loose. They lunged at arms and legs, barking and snapping as people stumbled backwards. A couple of the wolves got hold of coat sleeves and pant legs, tearing away strips of cloth as their victims ran away. The hellephants marched forward and herded the rest of the caravan up against the rock.

Mendel looked for Gooder and saw him a short distance away, trapped under a net. Capri signalled for her crew to stop fighting. They all stood together around Sir H. and Mendel, shielding them from Don Clapstone's view. The boy felt helpless. He looked up at Sir H. The alchemist pulled him close.

A loud shriek made everyone cover their ears. It was the horses. They all whinnied strangely, like high-pitched sirens. Their backs and necks were flexed hard against the nets with the strength of their call. Don Clapstone signalled to his agents. The men and women took leather straps and tied each horse's muzzle shut.

Once all of the horses were silent, the Don stood in front of the group and addressed them.

"You may all think you are righteous protectors, but really you are just striving to reconcile Mostly's mistake. No one will ever be able to make up for what he did to us!"

Capri's people all stepped forward, their hands balled into tight fists, but the wolves pulled at their leashes and barked fiercely, causing everyone to step back.

"Now! Give me Duffy!"

Mendel clutched Sir H.'s hand.

"Horus," said Don Woolstrum, who had appeared by his side with Pfeifer. The girl held a young wolf by its harness. "There's no need to use such intimidation. I'm sure this can be done peaceably."

"And what do you propose?" snapped Don Clapstone.

"A mature conversation, of course." She moved closer to the group. "Please understand, we all want the same thing. That is the safety of our world. No one wants to relive the past. Our Regula is here to protect us, and *they* should be the ones to protect us from the threat of the Putrid's Heart."

"All you Regula people care about is power over one another," retorted Capri. "And a Putrid's Heart would just be another pawn in your power games."

"Your conversation is pointless, Woolstrum," said Don

Clapstone. He gestured to two agents. "Go and retrieve Duffy." The Don reached into his pocket and pulled out a vial of clear liquid. "I'll get the stone and a full confession myself."

The two men stepped toward the group, but everyone stood shoulder to shoulder. Mendel didn't know what to do. He felt his body flush with the heat of panic. Esther slithered up to his shoulder. She seemed relaxed. Mendel heard her quiet voice say 'help is here.' He was confused. Who was coming? he asked her, but he couldn't understand her reply. He looked to Sir H. and was even more puzzled to see a smile on his face. His mentor winked at him. A shadow passed over them. Sir H. pointed at the sky.

Mendel looked up. It took him a moment to figure out what he saw. Bodies. Teeth. Wings.

"Pegasuses!" he shouted without meaning to.

There were shouts, hellephant trumpets, wolf howls and loud whinnies. The pegasi were freeing the horses! They swooped down and slashed at the nets and bindings. The horses leapt free and ran to aid their human companions, who had scattered to join the fight. Some of the flying horses swarmed the hellephants, making them rear. Agents rolled down the hellephants' backs to the ground, where Capri's people pinned and restrained them. Agents released the wolves, and they jumped onto the backs of the horses, but the pegasi grabbed them by their scruffs with their front talons and flung them to the edge of the cliff. Most of the wolves abandoned the agents and slunk down the mountainside, tails tucked.

Capri ran to Sir H., who leaned against the rock face, wheezing.

"We've got to get the stone out of here!" She held him under one arm while Mendel held the other, and the three of them hobbled to the path toward Kapathia.

A hard forced knocked Mendel to the ground. He felt claws digging into his back and a heavy weight pushing all of the air out of his lungs. Wet breath hit the back of his neck. He didn't think he'd ever breathe again, but at last the weight lifted. Mendel rolled onto his back. Pfeifer and her wolf stood over him. She struggled to hold it back.

Capri was being held by Don Woolstrum and another agent. Don Clapstone struggled with Sir H. on the ground. Mendel tried to get up, but Pfeifer loosened her grip on her wolf, and it snapped at his face, causing him to fall backwards. A hellephant loomed over them.

Don Clapstone tore at Sir H.'s jacket. The alchemist's face was bright red and his hair was soaked with sweat. His face was twisted in pain, but he fought hard against the Don and managed to keep the man's hands away from his inside pocket. But Mendel saw the agony on his face, and knew he couldn't defend himself for much longer.

Someone screamed. The boy looked over and saw Butter wrapped around Don Woolstrum's head. Felda clung to the back of the other agent and pulled him off her mother. Capri ran to Sir H. and pushed Don Clapstone hard. The man tumbled into Pfeifer's wolf, surprising it, and it bit the Don's arm, making him yell. Pfeifer pulled the animal off him. Capri tried to help Sir H. to his feet, but the hellephant charged them. They covered their faces as the giant beast raised a clawed hand, ready to strike, but the blow never landed.

Gooder charged up behind the hellephant and tore at its

back leg. A pegasus flew down and slashed at the monster's face. It trumpeted wildly and grabbed at the flying horse, but she was too quick for it. The chestnut horse joined Gooder and slashed at the beast's back leg. The hellephant yelled a husky cry, ducked its head and lumbered back the way it came.

The flying horse landed right next to Mendel and regarded him for a brief moment. She was dark purple, so dark she looked black. Only when she moved a certain way in the light could he see the purple. She whickered at him and flew away.

Mendel watched her go, but shouting brought his attention back to the ground. Don Clapstone and Sir H. were grappling over the black coin purse, tugging it back and forth between them. Gooder rushed in and knocked into the Don, making him fly backward. The boy's heart dropped like a rock into his stomach as the purse flew high into the air, soaring out toward the edge of the cliff.

Suddenly, something bizarre happened to Mendel. The world went dim and time slowed down. The strange silver equations appeared. They were written on the ground, up in the air and followed the flying stone. He somehow knew what the equation was telling him. It was calculating. It said that if he ran at this speed and jumped this high, he would catch the bag. His mind tried to worry about falling down the mountain, but the symbols told him that his feet would land on the ground. Mendel didn't know why, but he trusted the equations.

He broke into a run, and only saw his path to saving the stone from being lost, nothing else. The symbols changed as he moved, directing him and telling him what to compensate for, such as the slight incline of the ground. He felt fast and strong and sure. As he reached the edge of the cliff he saw the purse above him beyond the edge of the plateau, dropping away. With all of his strength, he leapt into the air and reached out. He saw that the bag was a little too far away, and he didn't have enough momentum to grab it. But the symbols still predicted that he would catch it. Just as he began to doubt himself, Esther slipped out the end of his sleeve, wrapped herself around his wrist and stretched across the gap, grabbing the stone. A smile spread across his face, but then, as he felt the hard pull of gravity, the smile left and was replaced by fear. He looked down and saw a dark abyss of jagged rock. His arms and legs flailed. He was falling.

Time resumed, and he heard Sir H.'s pained shout. His heart was in his throat, he couldn't scream. The wind cut his face and the view of the mountains quickly changed. Black rock closed in on him. His breath was gone and his entire body felt cold. He was still falling but he felt as though he had already died. *The thought* laughed a dark laugh that filled his mind in a drowning flood. The equation's prediction was wrong. Most of the symbols had faded away, only a few remained, the ones that told him his feet would land safely on the ground. Mendel shut his eyes and waited for the end.

He felt a sharp pinch in his shoulders, and his whole body abruptly jerked upward. He opened his eyes, but didn't understand what was happening. The mountains were getting farther away instead of closer. His shoulders really hurt. He looked up. The dark purple pegasus had caught him with her front talons. She flew away from the mountain with the rest of her flock. Mendel couldn't turn to see behind him. He looked down. Another pegasus flew below him. She was dark brown with black wings. The horse holding him lowered him down onto the other's back and let go, he landed with a thump. He was riding the brown pegasus.

He turned and saw the plateau far behind them. The flock flew over the mountains above the path that followed the ridge to Kapathia. The cold air stung his face, but he didn't care. He looked down at Esther. She was wrapped around his hand and the purse. He thanked her, and then he thanked the pegasus he rode. She tilted her head slightly.

A dozen pegasi made up the flock. The dark purple horse flew at the front and neighed commands. The entire group shifted in unison. Their large wingspans blotted out the scenery below. Mendel could see different patterns and designs in their feathers.

The sun disappeared and was replaced by moonlight. After an hour of flight, the flock landed on a large mountain plateau covered in lavender-grey fields of ladyheather. Carved into the ridges of black rock face were tall, multi-storied houses with warm lights shining from round windows. Strings of light globes decorated narrow paths and stairways that traversed the town. Families climbed down ladders that hung from doors, and ran to greet him. The villagers gaped at the sight of Mendel on a pegasus' back, though they approached the flock with comfortable familiarity.

The brown pegasus shifted uncomfortably. Mendel heard Esther say 'get off.' He obliged and awkwardly tumbled over her wing and onto the ground, landing on his backside. One of the villagers helped him up, and by time he got to his feet the pegasus had wandered into the field with the rest of her flock.

Mendel recounted the battle on the mountain and his flight on the pegasus to a crowd of people, gesticulating excitedly.

An hour later the caravan caught up to him. Horses and Capri's people poured out of the narrow path opening and into the fields. A break in the crowd of villagers and animals revealed a laboring Sir H. The alchemist caught sight of Mendel and rushed painfully over to him, falling to his knees and hugging him tight.

"Oh my boy!" Sir H. was crying. "Oh my darling boy. I thought I'd lost you."

"The Primore symbols told me I could catch the stone and land on the ground." Mendel smiled brightly and handed the purse to Sir H.

"You done good, lad." He held him tightly.

"I flew on a pegasus, Sir H."

"Of course you did. A Primore doin' such an unusual fing only makes sense." He laughed, gave a great sniff and messed the boy's hair.

The tired, sweating horses whinnied and trotted to the pasture where the pegasi were settled for the night. Gooder stopped to check on Sir H., but he was clearly distracted by the females and kept almost knocking the man over with affectionate nudges. Finally Sir H. told him to leave off, and the horse galloped into the field with the rest of his species.

"Welcome to Kapathia," said Capri. She hugged them both.

"Why did those pegasi come to help us, Capri?" asked Mendel.

"This flock has used our pasture to deliver their young for generations. When it's time to fly away, the female foals go with them, while the males are left behind. Our horses are their sons. They heard the call of our boys and came to defend their blood."

The Great Lady

"Those are some powerful allies to 'ave," said Sir H.

Mendel saw the pain in Sir H.'s face and gave him his shoulder to lean on. The man winced as they walked forward.

"Come, Henny. I know you're eager to see the Great Lady more than ever, but you need to rest and eat first." Capri sidled up on Sir H.'s other side and helped him toward a house with a ground level entrance.

"I'm not going to argue wif you, Capri. My bones are aching."

Esther slithered down to the ground and snaked her way through the grass alongside Mendel. He pointed at a large congregation of blackbirds perched on the windowsills and rooftops of the mountain homes. "What kind of birds are those, Sir H.?"

Capri answered. "Those are mountain ravens. We've developed a symbiotic relationship with them. The ravens bring us lichen and berries that grow on the mountainsides, and we let them nest in and around our homes for safety. Blackened raptors are very dangerous and will kill ravens for sport."

One of the birds landed on Capri's shoulder and cawed. "This is Chepi. She and I have been friends since she was a fledgling." The bird pecked at rips in her clothes and cawed with concern. "She loves to look after me."

They helped Sir H. into the small but welcoming house. The kitchen was compact and shared a space with the sitting area. Carved into the back wall was a ladder that led upward to the second story. They set Sir H. down in a soft chair by the fireplace. Capri pulled out a wooden chair from a nearby table and gestured for Mendel to sit down. Felda came in carrying chunks of coal and fed them into the fire. She had a smile on her face.

"What a good fight that was!" She looked at Mendel. "You didn't get to see my mother wallop Clapstone right in the face."

Capri tried not to smile. "We would have all been done for if it weren't for you and Butter. Clapstone almost had that purse open. If he caught sight of the stone they would have grounds to pursue charges." Felda embraced her mother. Capri's eyes welled up.

"Mendel is the one that saved us all." Felda released her mother and messed his hair. "You made every heart stop beating, even the Advanced Discipline ninnies, going over the cliff like you did."

"The symbols told me that my feet would land safely on the ground," said Mendel.

Capri and Sir H. exchanged looks.

"Any sign of 'em comin' after us?" asked Sir H.

"No," replied Felda. "They were pretty scattered. And since they never set eyes on the stone we reckon they won't have any ground to justify their attack. I'm helping draw up the law papers to send to the Regula at first light to establish our case. The Disciplines will put up a fight and use their advisory committee connections, but so will we."

"Good work, my love," said Capri. A tear rolled down her cheek. Felda smiled and wiped it away.

Capri sniffed and said, "Can you fill the pot with water and put it over the fire so we can feed these boys?"

Felda left the small room with a skip in her step, and returned shortly with a bucket of water that she dumped into a big black kettle. Capri stood at a stone counter, opening containers and jars, and preparing food to cook. "Can you cut some meat and bone off a deer in the hut?" Felda disappeared again. Mendel heard Sir H.'s stomach growl, and his own stomach grumbled in reply. The two looked at each other and smiled. They hadn't eaten anything since the stew they had had early that morning.

"You're in for a treat, my boy. Blackened deer meat is the tastiest."

Mendel thought for a moment. "If they hunt deer for meat, why didn't the deer we saw on the slopes run from us?"

"Sharp boy." Sir H. winked. "Those weren't the same species as the comestible class of Blackened deer. The retavic species belong to the canny class."

"And the people of the mountains have a pact with the retavic," said Capri. "They are very intelligent, and would make a formidable enemy."

"What happens if people break the pact?"

Capri smiled. "The retavic are capable of war. I would hate to be on the wrong side of that fight."

"How do you tell the difference between the retavic and Blackened deer?" asked Mendel.

"Despite their name, Blackened deer have golden coats and pale yellow antlers. They are much smaller too."

Mendel quickly scribbled into his imagination. He got distracted when Felda returned with a leg of blackened deer meat that she threw straight into the pot. Mendel's mouth watered. Capri added an assortment of vegetables, spice cubes and herbs. The fire warmed the room, and the air smelled savory. Sir H. nodded off, snoring softly. The caravan woman with the strawberry hair entered the house with their gear, which she left in a pile next to Sir H.'s chair. The alchemist woke briefly and quickly nodded off again.

Butter jumped in through an open window, paced back and forth in front of the stew pot and harassed Capri with a series of meows. She finally threw a piece of meat to the cat, and she handed another to Esther, who was curled up in Mendel's lap.

A little while later the food was ready. Capri woke Sir H. and placed a bowl of thick dark stew in his hands. She put a smaller bowl on the floor next to Mendel, and Esther slithered off his lap and buried her face in it. Butter protested and was quickly quieted with his own bowl. Finally Capri handed Mendel his portion. The boy was so hungry he didn't wait for the meat to cool, and he burned the roof of his mouth. The meat was tender, juicy and greasy. The vegetables were starchy and sweet, the spices and herbs fragrant and savory. The weary travelers finished quickly. Capri came around and dished out seconds.

Butter passed out in front of the fire with a full belly. He purred deeply as Esther groomed her way through his thick orange coat. The boy started to fall asleep in his chair, but then Sir H.'s voice snapped him awake.

"We better descend soon, otherwise me and the boy will likely 'ave to be carried back up."

"Let me fetch some globes." Capri opened a large trunk.

"Descend? I thought we had to ascend to the Great Lady?"

"We 'ave to ascend to Kapathia, where the entrance to 'er ladyship's 'ome is. But the passageway descends into the mountain a ways."

Capri handed a large light globe stick to each of them. "Follow me."

Mendel picked up the strangers staff from their pile of belongings and helped Sir H. out of his chair.

"Here. Use this," he said, handing Sir H. the staff.

Esther slithered up Mendel's arm and draped herself around his shoulders. He was grateful for the warmth she provided against the mountain chill.

They followed Capri out of the house with their globes alight, and she took them along a dark wall for several paces to a narrow crevice in the rock face. It was pitch dark inside. The light showed a short tunnel of rough, jagged walls. At the end of it, a misshapen doorway revealed a staircase that led downward into the mountain.

"Watch your step," murmured Capri.

Mendel held onto the wall with one hand while lighting his way with the globe. Capri stopped at the more degraded sets of stairs and helped the boy and injured man negotiate their way past uneven and loose steps. Mendel had an excellent sense of direction above ground, but he was lost inside the mountain. He tried to imagine who this mysterious woman was and why she would live down here.

A half hour later, the rocky staircase ended in a large cave. Mendel held his globe up. A still body of water extended from their feet across the cave floor. Sharp teeth of dripping rock covered the high ceiling. A narrow strip of land cut across the underground pond. Capri led them along the island path. After several dozen paces, the path ended at the back of the cave on a small mound of land. There was no one there.

Mendel looked around, confused. He noticed a small tunnel in the wall of the cave. Mendel figured he could fit inside it, but didn't think it would be comfortable. He wondered if the mysterious woman was a small girl.

Capri made a barking noise toward the tunnel. Sir H. put his arm around Mendel and Esther. The gusselsnuff sniffed the air frantically. Mendel started to think that maybe the mysterious Great Lady was not a woman at all. But he wasn't sure what tunneled through mountains.

He heard scraping and clinking noises coming from the dark opening, like metal on rock. He stood on his toes, leaning forward in anticipation. What looked like a metal snout poked out of the tunnel entrance.

"It's an ore badger!" exclaimed Mendel.

Capri smiled, and Sir H. squeezed the boy's shoulder. "Mendel, my boy, I'd like you to meet the Great Lady. She's one of the few ore badgers left in our world, and it's up to us to protect 'er kind."

The Great Lady took tentative steps out of the tunnel. Silver scales covered her large, long body, and they glittered in the light. Her front claws gleamed and clicked as she walked on the hard ground. Capri approached her and knelt down. The Great Lady looked in her direction, though not directly at her. Mendel remembered that ore badgers were blind. She sat back on her haunches and bowed her head towards them. Capri bowed back.

Mendel took a step closer.

"How do you communicate with her?" he asked.

Both Capri and the Great Lady turned their heads and looked at Mendel.

"Communicating with the badgers is simpler than with people. There are a series of sounds that we exchange that have simple meanings," explained Capri. "For instance—" Capri made a few chirping noises, and the Great Lady chirped back. "I told her I'm here with others and that we are friendly. She replied that she is alone and friendly."

Mendel paid close attention to the sounds they made and scribbled excitedly in the air. The two females exchanged another series of chirps and barks.

"I asked after her kin, and the Great Lady replied they are hidden deep down and all are safe and healthy," explained Capri. They had another exchange. "I asked her about the movements of the beasts down below. She said they are searching nowhere near our world, but they are searching aggressively."

Then Capri gestured for Sir H. to step forward, and she chirped some more. Mendel saw that the alchemist was sweating quite a bit. The boy put a hand on his arm to reassure him. Sir H. extracted the coin purse and pulled out the Putrid's Heart. The sight of the object made everyone hold their breath and clutch their stomachs. Sir H. shook slightly. Mendel felt dizzy. The Great Lady didn't seem bothered by the stone, though. When Sir H. handed it to her, she merely cupped it with her back claw that she then kept close to her body and under a plate of armor.

They showed her the stranger's staff. She sniffed, nibbled and scratched at it, and nudged it back to Sir H. after giving a few short barks.

"She said she doesn't know what it is, but she will ask her kin," said Capri.

The Great Lady bowed her head and chirped. Capri and Sir H. did the same, and Mendel mimicked the gesture. The ore badger turned her head toward the boy and seemed to study him for a moment. Then she disappeared back into the tunnel.

"Where is she going to take the stone, Sir H.?"

"Somewhere deep below. Where it belongs," he answered.

"Why didn't we give her both stones?"

"Because if someone were to get a stone and break it open on our surface, callin' the beasts, then we will need another one to make them leave."

Mendel listened to the distance clink of the Great Lady fade into silence.

Capri put a hand on Mendel's shoulder. "You're a remarkable boy, Mendel. Our community is lucky to have you, and I feel you will do important things for us and this world." She bent down and hugged him.

"I won't let anyone down. I promise." Mendel heard Sir H. sniffle. The two embraced, and Esther wrapped herself around them both.

Sir H. released the boy and wiped his eyes. "We best start back up. We are all in need of a good, deep sleep."

It took twice as long to ascend the stairs, but eventually they emerged. Mendel deeply inhaled the fresh, chilling air. A brilliant starscape glittered across a black and purple sky. He saw the lights of other small towns scattered throughout the mountains. Sir H. put his arm around Mendel.

"This is one of me most favorite places."

"I think it's one of mine, too."

They stood in comfortable silence for a moment. Then a

number of thoughts bubbled to the surface of Mendel's mind all at once.

"The stranger is on the opposite side of our quest, isn't she, Sir H.? She'll keep after the stones just as much as we will protect them, won't she?"

The alchemist thought for a moment. "I reckon so. But it's important we stay 'ead of 'er. Back 'ome in the Northern Forests, in me village, there is a Primore. Magda. She's very old, if she's still alive. She might be able to tell us somefin' 'bout the stranger."

"Can we go there next?" asked Mendel excitedly.

Sir H. chuckled. "No. There are only two ways into the forests. One is the Sinking River, which won't be crossable til next year. The other is the Sidian Lava Lands that won't cool off til mid-winter, and even then it's still dangerous to cross."

Mendel frowned. "Will we go back to Abylant then?"

Sir H. smiled. "Only for a short while. We'll be livin' in Manuva before you know it."

The idea of living at the academy made his stomach flutter. "But what about the Advanced Disciplines people? They won't leave us alone either, will they?"

"No, but that's a battle that's been goin' on for ages. We know how to fight a good fight. As you saw today."

Mendel tried to find that comforting, but something deep inside told him that things were shifting. How and in what way he could not say.

"Come on. Let's find beds and get some sleep." Sir H. and the boy limped towards Capri's house.

Mendel took one last look at the sky. A great emotion grew out from his heart and filled every corner of his being. The best thoughts that ever occupied his mind occupied it all at once. He belonged to a community that accepted who he was. Next year he would be studying at the academy, with his closest friend, and no limits set upon what he could learn. So many exciting questions piled up in his head, and he could hardly wait to start exploring them.

Regardless of the dangers that lurked around them, he felt the power of his community as a force to be reckoned with. They had many allies, friends and companions. A solid connection woven between them all. Because of that bond, the last stone was safely delivered to a unique creature, the Advanced Disciplines agents were defeated and had retreated, and the stranger in all her unknown power had been overcome.

Mendel felt optimistic about their world. Not only was it safe, it was flourishing.

Acknowledgements

And now I need to thank the village that raised my novel. Thanks to Aimee H. for suggesting I go darker with the pixie fight scene. Thanks to Sandy D. for helping me decide which novel to work on. I'm very grateful to my brother-in-law Adam, who did such a diligent and thorough job with his edits, making the book so much better. I also need to thank Adam's awesome mom, Gloria. She proofread my entire manuscript with short notice in just a couple of days. A big thanks to my sisters Kathleen and Elizabeth for proofreading my book. When I asked them to do it, neither one hesitated to say yes. To my twin sister and wombmate, Martha, for being so unconditionally supportive. One phone call with her and the wind was back in my sails. Thanks to my brother Peter for being an ogre, I love you. To my mother and Jim, thanks for taking me in that summer before I began my MFA. It gave me the time and space to conjure up the idea for *The Alchemist's Theorem*. And thanks to my father. I love that over that past few years we have become philosophy buddies; we have the best conversations. Also, his support has been paramount to getting me this far. And a giant thank you to Mista Brooks. This guy came into my life and changed everything. Because of him this book is at its best, I'm at my best, and my life is at its happiest.

Thank You

I am deeply grateful to everyone who backed and promoted my Kickstarter campaign. I received a great deal of support from caring friends, dedicated family, and valiant samaritans.

A sincere thanks to my family: the Chiavettas, the McGills, the Pericaks, the Karnes, the Pecks, the Thompsons, and the Lebermans. I love being a part of this giant collective. Also, thanks to the town of Brant community. And a special thanks to Peter Chiavetta, Morag and Jim Levin, Elizabeth Chiavetta and Adam Lattman for their extremely generous pledges.

A mighty thanks to my friends as well as Brooks' friends. It was so enriching to hear from so many of you, especially those with whom I haven't been in touch for a while. Thank you Karen T., Wael B., Jason Coe and Sally Peck for your kindhearted support. Thank you Craig Engler for all of your advice. A special thanks to Neil for his incredibly generous pledge. A giant thank you to Jerry Friends.

A big thanks to all the wonderful samaritans who backed me. You are all so special to me. Every time I saw a supporter's name that I did not recognize, my heart swelled with gratitude. You're the best.